*un*conventional
BUSINESS meets *PLEASURE*

KENNY *WRIGHT*

KW PUBLISHING

www.kennywriter.com

Unconventional: Business Meets Pleasure

Edited by Lucy V. Morgan and Summer Wright

Cover design by Kenny Wright

Cover image © Ross Petukhov/Bigstock.com

First digital edition electronically published by KW Publishing, October 2013

First print edition published by KW Publishing, November 2013

Printed by CreateSpace, Charleston SC

Introduction

It was on the flight out to the Health & Fitness Convention that I really noticed Linnea Sorenson. I mean, I had always thought that she was attractive in a corporate, pantsuit, take-no-shit-from-anyone kind of way. It was hard not to notice cheekbones like hers, particularly when her light blonde hair was always twisted into a high bun.

Thing was, to me, the attractive executive was more like someone who my parents would have over to dinner than someone I'd hit on at a bar. She attended meetings that lasted all day. She had a wardrobe of tailored blouses and matching accessories. She had a husband and teenage children. She was an Adult, with a capital A.

Me? Well, I'm in my mid-twenties. Need I say more? I spend my weekends in bars and clubs. I drink too much, play too hard, and happily pay for it most of the week.

At the back of the plane, watching the slow progression of passengers claim their cramped seats, I saw her, but didn't recognize her. Not at first. I was too wrapped up in the people watching. This always fascinated me. Most travelers treated the plane like it was their living room.

They wore things that I'd never dream of wearing in public. Sweats. Track suits. Pajama bottoms with gray hoodies. There were a few business travelers in their suits, a few people in nothing more offensive than a jacket and jeans. And then there was her.

She was dressed for comfort, like everyone else, but managed to pull it off without looking sloppy. She wore black yoga pants and a loose black top that hung low enough to show off smooth, unblemished shoulders of creamy skin and a suggestion of small, well-formed breasts.

It wasn't until she was just a few rows down that I recognized her. I kept looking, thinking that this woman merely looked like Linnea, the way certain people look like celebrities at just the right angle in just the right light. She wore her blonde hair in a high ponytail that didn't seem right for Mrs. Sorenson, had on almost no make-up, and looked shorter than the Director of Marketing. She looked…normal.

Yet I couldn't deny those cheekbones. It was her. And after two years of working with her without noticing her, I *noticed*.

"This is a nice surprise. How's it going, Adam?"

Any doubt that it was her was gone with that Finnish accent. Sweet. Sexy, even. But no nonsense. I wondered if she used the same tone to praise that she did to berate.

"Good to see you, too, Linnea." Her name felt weird as it rolled off my tongue. Like I should be addressing her as something more respectful: *missus* or *miss*. First names felt too familiar.

"This your first time flying to Las Vegas?" she asked.

"My very first. You?"

She lifted her roller bag into the overhead compartment, her voice straining as she replied. "I've been to HFC for the past few years."

Her loose black top rose as she stretched, revealing the delicious expanse of smooth skin. I checked out her ass, not two feet from my face. It was a work of art, round and tight. Encased in skin tight yoga pants, I couldn't see any panty lines.

She pulled out her phone and speed dialed someone, dismissing me with a smile.

"Honey, I just boarded…yes, I will…" She laughed. "Okay, I'll keep that in mind. Bye…I love you, too."

Her husband. I wondered what kind of man she'd married. Probably someone broad-shouldered and square-jawed, who could give as much as Linnea did. I imagined loud, angry fights and wild make up sex.

She offered me a smile, launching back into our previous conversation like she hadn't just made a phone call—and I hadn't just been picturing her having sex.

"This'll be the first time I'm bringing an on-site tech team, though." She spoke around the stream of people coming in and settling into their seats. "I've asked for one every year since I started, so you guys better not make me look bad."

She said it with a smile, but I got the feeling that she wasn't kidding about her expectation. Being on the "tech team," I'd never had much reason to interact with Mrs. Sorenson, but her reputation as the Director of Ice preceded her.

"Casey and I are the best. You can count on us."

She didn't even acknowledge me, like what I'd said was such a given that it wasn't necessary to be spoken. "Do you know why I'm bringing you?"

"To help man our booth on the showroom floor?"

Linnea shook her head. "Any intern could do that. No, I brought you because of *Jetson*."

It made me smile to hear someone in senior management use the codename that we developers used. *Jetson* was our latest (and greatest, in my opinion) software for treadmills, ellipticals, and stationary bikes—named after the futuristic family who rode moving walk-ways everywhere—and it was our flagship product at HFC.

"So you're bringing us as a reward?"

The Director of Ice had a musical laugh. "I'm not sure that you'll think it's a reward by the end of the week. The days are long and it's not glamorous work. You'll probably spend most of the time assisting the sales staff, and any technical issues you will probably be troubleshooting."

"Is it too late to de-board?"

Linnea smiled, and it did crazy things to those European cheeks of hers. "Like I'd let you."

Our eyes locked. This woman was used to getting her way. I started to reform my idea of what her husband was like. "So you want me… to stay?"

What are you doing? Flirting with the boss?

Linnea's gaze lingered, her reply caught on the tip of her pink tongue. What would that feel like, pushing into my mouth? She was probably a hard kisser…

"You think you're good, but you're not great. Not yet. I wanted you and Casey there because I wanted the minds behind *Jetson* to see how our customers use it. It's a good product, but not the best. Not yet."

That prickled. Says her. There was no better product out there. No sense in arguing intricacies like that, though. The captain came on and announced that we were cleared for take-off. She kept watching me as the flight attendant rambled through the emergency procedures. Are you going to say something?

She wasn't my boss—not technically—but for the next week she'd serve as one. Did I really want to start it off on such a bad note?

Linnea's stare broke as our flight attendant passed by, checking belts.

"Too late to de-board. Looks like you're stuck with me."

"I can think of worse things."

Linnea laughed at my hammy line and I felt a little disappointed in myself. I was smoother than that. She pulled her copy of *US Weekly* from the seat pocket in front of her. Our conversation was over. I'd been dismissed.

I watched her on and off through the flight. Her severe demeanor melted as she nodded off, celebrity rag limp in her lap. Like I said before, there was no denying that Linnea Sorenson was a beautiful woman—the same way the pages of *Vanity Fair* are filled with beautiful women. But she'd always been about as real as one of those glossy pages.

Only sleeping and vulnerable, I saw the woman her husband saw. Or her friends. Or a chick I'd happily take back to my apartment for some fun. Her blouse had slipped off her shoulder, revealing smooth skin and the slim strap of a pale pink bra. She had a tight, athletic body that probably looked fantastic naked.

Director of Ice. Fuck would I love to melt her. Just for one night.

I thought about her conversation with her husband before take-off. I glanced at the large diamond on her left hand. The asshole in me wondered if that guy gave her what she needed, and guessed that he did not. My better half said it didn't matter—she was another man's, and that was a barrier I'd never crossed.

We were headed to Las Vegas, city of sin. No sense dwelling on what I could never have. I looked one last time at Linnea, at her bra strap and the way her blonde ponytail followed the pointed ridge of her jaw.

C'est la vie. I think that meant: there were other hotties to be had.

chapter one

We touched down in Las Vegas just after sunset. The plane banked once over the Strip, its electric boulevard lined with glowing casinos all trying to outdo one another for fantastic extravagance. I felt like I was flying into a dream—pyramids next to New York City skyscrapers—and even the architecture looked ready to party.

Against that backdrop, even sharing a taxi with my boss couldn't dull the hum of excitement I felt.

"So are you going to go out tonight? Hit the clubs?" Linnea asked.

It was weird—like having a conversation about strip clubs with my aunt. "I hadn't planned on it." I hadn't. "Maybe check out some casinos. You?"

"Room service and sleep for me. You have fun."

The hotel where we were staying was actually a block off the main drag, a smaller and more affordable place to stay. Despite it not boasting a casino, though, the lobby still rang with the clatter and chime of slot machines eating money.

Linnea and I split up at check-in, where she slid into the preferred member line and I was stuck at the back of a bunch of tourists. Pulling out my iPhone, I started checking up on what I'd missed on Facebook as I waited when I felt a tap on my shoulder.

"Flying in with the boss," came a cheerful voice. "How was that?"

I turned to the familiar face smiling up at me behind dark-rimmed glasses.

"Hey, Case. Good to see you!"

I felt the urge to hug my coworker, like I hadn't seen her in ages, rather than just last Friday.

Casey laughed, returning my enthusiasm with a sarcastic version of her own. "Good to see you, too, Adam! Long time. How have you been, man?"

I held up my hand. "Okay, okay. It's just weird, seeing you outside of the office, you know?"

"Don't recognize me in my civilian clothes?" She stepped back and posed in her cropped jeans and short-sleeved blouse—which, unlike Linnea, Casey had worn many times into the office.

"I don't recognize you without the baggy gray hoodie."

"I could go get it from my room if it'll help."

I shook my head. "You know what I mean. We're a long way from Philly."

"Now *that* is true." She looked over at Linnea, who was already through the line and on her way to the elevators. "Hey, remember when we thought she was going to fire us?"

When Linnea Sorenson had called Casey and I into her office last month, it was the first time either of us had ever stepped onto that floor, and neither of us knew what to expect. We'd heard rumors of a high turnover rate in the Marketing Department, and while it didn't make sense that we'd be let go by another executive, irrationally, we both jumped to that conclusion.

I laughed. "I'm pretty sure it was *you* who thought that."

"Uh, huh. I saw your face, Adam. You looked like you were going to vomit."

I looked around, ignoring the quip in favor of the ring of the slot machines. "Pretty crazy turn of events since then, huh?"

"Between being unemployed and being sent to Las Vegas? You're wise beyond your years, Adam."

"Har, har."

"Next!" the hotel attendant behind the counter called.

"Well, I better check in. See you later?"

Casey offered a non-committal nod. "Maybe. I've been here since this morning and have been lying out in the sun most of the day. I'm pretty beat."

"You? Lying out in the sun?"

"I know, right? Me, doing something *outside*!" She rolled her eyes. "There's a lot about me that you don't know, mister, and I happen to tan pretty well."

Now that she mentioned it, her face and arms held a nice, golden hue.

"Sir? Are you ready?" the attendant asked with an impatient smile.

"Yes, sorry." To Casey: "Well, maybe I'll see you tonight. Otherwise, tomorrow on the floor."

"Bye, Adam."

There was something coy about the way she turned and left, but I couldn't put my finger on it. Instead, my focus dipped to her ass, held tight and taut in her snug jeans. I'd always found Casey cute—and on a few occasions, had wondered what it'd be like to hook up with her—but she wasn't really my type. She was too…she was too Casey.

I shook the thoughts away and wheeled my bags up to the desk. Las Vegas was filled with *my type*—the kind that came without strings and that I could say goodbye to in the morning.

****

The Health & Fitness Convention was one of the largest of its kind in the nation. Vendors from all over the country came to attend workshops on best practices in health and fitness, latest trends, and the newest technologies (this is where we came in). Not surprisingly, almost everyone was fit, and more than a few were really attractive.

The booth next to us was some kind of yoga studio/yoga school. Every time I started to figure it out, I got distracted by one of the *yogis* demonstrating a technique that seemed designed to show off the perfection of her body.

"Any questions?" Linnea Sorenson asked, drawing me back to her pep talk. I'd caught the gist of it: be polite, smile, make eye contact, take information, and excellent customer service above everything else.

Director Sorenson was back with her hair in its tight coil and her tailored pantsuit, provocative yet professional. And most important of all, her attitude was all business. With my mind still in the gutter from the modified version of down dog being demonstrated just behind her, I wondered what Linnea was wearing under her suit. Something lacy, I imagined, a matched bra and thong that would look great on the floor of my hotel room—

"Something to say, Mr. Murphy?" Linnea asked. She'd misinterpreted my long stare for a question.

"Be helpful. Smile. Scan convention badges. Got it."

"Very perceptive."

Was I imagining that twinkle in her eye?

"Well, then I'll leave the coordination up to Chuck." She nodded at her second-in-command, who stepped up with a clipboard and pen. "We're going to have a great week, guys. Thanks in advance."

I watched her disappear down the exhibit hall. Yes, definitely a thong…if anything at all.

"You don't have the hots for the boss, do you Adam?" Casey asked beside me once Linnea was gone.

"Hmm?"

Casey wore the black polo with our logo emblazoned on her impressive bust. Not that our booth uniforms were particularly salacious, but they were a lot more distracting on her than on any of the guys present.

"What? Hello? Up here, Adam." She snapped her fingers, getting me to look at her face.

"I'm sorry, what now?"

Casey rolled her eyes. "Have you always been such a guy?" She paused, then: "Yeah, you have."

"Hey, what can I say? You've worked with me for what? A year? Does this surprise you?"

"Not really—"

"Casey? Adam? I knew it was a good idea to split you two up," Chuck said. "Tech monkeys with the sales team. I want the expertise with the experience. Adam, you're with me on Team A."

"No surprise there," I grinned.

"Casey, you're B Team. A Team, we'll take the first shift. Doors open in…a half hour. Be back by nine."

Casey turned to me. "Have fun. I'm going to hit the blackjack tables!"

The first couple hours were pretty slow. Chuck and I spent more time answering each other's questions than other people's. Mostly, I was curious about what it was like working for Linnea, but his answers mostly affirmed my original assessment of her.

"She's really talented at what she does, but I can't say that I know much about her beyond work," he said. To pass the time, we'd taken to arranging our give-aways—blue wristbands that you could hang your keys off of when working out—into elaborate patterns on our draped table.

"No barbeques at her house on the weekends or anything like that?"

"No. She doesn't even bring her husband and family to the company picnics. She keeps the two very separate."

"Weird."

Chuck shrugged. "I suppose. Some people are just like that. Work is one thing. Family is another."

"So you think she's totally different with her husband? She goes home and is, like, some kind of Suzy Homemaker?"

We both got a laugh out of that. "Well, I didn't say that."

We chatted up a couple of women working the yoga booth next to us. Brooke and Avery were exactly the type I'd normally go for: early twenty-something hotties with long hair, hard bodies, and seize-the-day attitudes.

Maybe it was the conversation we'd just had, or maybe it was the plane flight over, but I couldn't help comparing them to Linnea. When I did, they seemed so shallow, the conversations empty. I didn't care about how amazing it was to do yoga in the desert at sunrise no more than they cared about the treadmill UX we were peddling, but we talked for a stupid amount of time about both.

"So maybe we'll see you guys out tonight?" Brooke (or was it Avery?) asked as Casey and a marketing guy who was paired with her arrived.

"We'll be there," Chuck answered for us.

Casey sized up the situation quickly, a smirk already appearing on her face.

"Where will we be?" she asked.

Chuck answered. "Avery—" So it was Avery! "—here was just telling us about some hot spots they heard about tonight. What do you say, Case, you like dancing?"

I almost started laughing when my nerdy coworker—who I'd been working side-by-side with for close to a year now—lit up and nodded. "I love dancing!"

I couldn't stop myself from blurting out a *really?*

"Yeah. What? Just because I know C# and get excited by new jQuery releases doesn't mean I can't have fun in other ways."

My mind went to sex. With a line like that, how could it not? That realization that the cute coder with the black-framed glasses was more than a sitcom archetype? That.

It was too much for me in the moment. I realized that the jet lag was getting to me and if I was going to meet up with Brooke and Avery later on, I was going to need to nap.

"Well, get the details from Brooke—"

"Avery," Avery corrected.

"—I'm going to crash for a few. Chuck, catch up with you at the blackjack tables over at MGM?"

"Sounds good to me. Later, man."

On my way out of the convention hall, I ran into Linnea, looking harried but gorgeous.

"Oh, hello there, Adam."

Why did her saying my name suddenly make my heart flutter like that?

"A guy from City Fitness didn't stop by, did he?"

"I think Chuck talked to someone from there during the lunch press. Tall, broad shoulders. Curly hair?"

"That's him." Her pulled together demeanor melted a little. I saw the girl that she had been before she was the woman. "Great. I'm close to landing a deal with them."

I had a buddy who worked at City Fitness. They had gyms up and down the East Coast, and rumors were that they were about to expand nationally. "I take it this'll be big?"

"Yeah, you could say that." She winked. "They want to revamp their exercise equipment without having to invest in brand new machines. They're extremely interested in *Jetson*. If this happens, it may be the biggest deal we've ever made." I liked hearing her use *we* as much as I liked the excitement that radiated from her.

"Anything I can do to help?" My jet lag had mysteriously vanished.

"Don't think so. Our product is good enough to sell itself." Ah, that felt good. Stretch. She turned to go, and then added, "But thanks for the offer."

She had a great smile.

****

The girl was hot. Hot in exactly the way I'd imagined a convention hook-up should be. The glittering bodice of her dress hugged the kind of tits you could lose yourself in, full and ripe and tanned. She was tall and blonde, and knew how to move her body to the driving club beat. I could close my eyes and imagine feeling that hard, yogi body against me in bed all night—yet when I did close my eyes and try to imagine it, the woman I kept thinking about was Linnea.

"What?" Avery asked. Or was it Brooke? "You seem distracted."

"Sorry, just jetlagged, maybe."

"Sounds like you need another drink."

The gorgeous blonde dragged me over to the bar and I quickly ordered another whiskey and Coke.

"So you and your friend, Chuck, are from the East Coast?"

"Yeah." I leaned back on the bar and surveyed the club. Strobe lights turned the dance floor into a stuttering movie, stark white against deep black. I caught Casey out there, pressed up against some stranger wearing a black spangled dress that threatened my conception of her as Nerd Girl. I fought the urge to go to her and defend her honor.

The blonde was talking to me again.

"I'm sorry, what was that?" I used the loud music as cover. This wasn't working out.

"Should I be jealous? You keep looking at that chick."

"Oh, sorry. No. We're friends—coworkers, really."

"Good."

Only one and a half days into this trip and my whole world had been thrown upside down—or at least the women in my world. Bizarro Casey. Linnea Sorenson. Was this Vegas at work, sexualizing people who I thought were above that, even to me?

I took a sip of my drink before realizing that I didn't want to finish it. It was too much, and all I wanted to do was crawl back to my hotel room and fall asleep. The full day of standing and my jet lag came racing up. I looked over at the blonde, and felt the same way about her as I did about my drink.

Seeing my spacy expression, the blonde said, "What?"

"I think I've had too much to drink. And the jet lag is finally getting to me."

"I can think of a few cures for jet lag," she said.

I groaned, knowing what I was turning down, but doing it anyway. "Excuse me, I better be going. I've got…I'm tired."

Avery touched my face. "You seem tired quite a bit. Maybe you've got mono."

I backed away, bumping into a circle of dancers. Someone spilled his drink on himself, protesting with a loud *hey*. I ignored him, stumbling out of the club before anyone could see or stop me. I wasn't used to being so off my game. Maybe I really was jet lagged.

Outside, my ears still ringing with the bass of the club, I took a slow stroll back to the hotel. The Strip was alive with people, whooping and drinking openly. I should have been one of them, making a fool of myself and happy to suffer the consequences tomorrow. That was my usual M.O., after all. So what was different tonight?

I watched a couple going hot and heavy against a tree that was being up-lit by whatever casino I was passing. He ran his hand up under her skirt and she threw her head back and sighed. Now that was Vegas, and that's what I'd imagined myself doing when I packed for this trip. Not walking back to my room alone, intent on an "early" bedtime.

Thing was, by the time I made it back to the hotel, I wasn't ready to go to sleep. I was too wired. Jack and Coke mixed with pretty girls and surreal situations tended to do that to me.

I crossed the lobby and got all the way up to my room before deciding that that's not where I wanted to be. The book of services opened to a photo of the Jacuzzi next to the indoor pool on the top level of the hotel. Out the windows, the Nevada desert stretched.

I decided to hit that up.

No one was at the front desk of the spa, although there were towels stacked up and the doors weren't locked. I didn't bother trying to figure out if the pool was technically closed. If it was, then the worst they could do was tell me to get out. When in Vegas, right?

I didn't see anyone on the way to the locker room, either, although the lights were still on. I changed into my trunks and began to wonder if I'd see anyone at all when I emerged into the pool proper. A single person was doing laps, her sleek body slicing through the otherwise still surface like a swan across a clear lake. She wore a black bikini designed for exercise and had a lean, slender body, but that was all I could tell and didn't want to stare. Besides, I wasn't here to pick up chicks; if I wanted that, I wouldn't have left the club.

The hot tub was against the far wall, set apart from the pool on a raised platform. The windows didn't show more than that night had fallen, although it still gave a sense of how high we were, despite the pool.

Not that it mattered. I wasn't here for the view. I was here for the Jacuzzi, which looked divine. When I sank into its roiling depths and felt the water pressure squeeze my ribs, it *felt* divine.

I spent most of my time sitting cross-legged on the floor of the tub, submerged up to my ears. My mind wandered everywhere, from the convention to blackjack systems to *Jetson* and how to improve its code. But mostly, they fixed on Linnea Sorenson. What was it about the blonde that captivated me so much? Her trim body? Her sexy professionalism, maybe? That accent?

A splashing sound across the pool drew me out of my musings. The swimmer pulled herself out of the pool, her head thrown back as water cascading around her. I blinked. She had long blonde hair that hung wet and straight between her shoulder blades. While the bikini was more practical than showy, it still clung to a tight ass that I recognized right away.

The woman padded across to her towel, dried her face, then wrapped it around her body. Any doubt that this was Linnea evaporated when she checked her phone and called someone.

"Sorry I missed your call."

Yup, sexy voice and all.

Before I could decide what to do, she strode toward the locker room on legs that were as long and lean as I'd imagined. "OK, I understand. We can customize the program to whatever specs you like. So talk it over with your bosses and let me know exactly what you need."

Linnea pulled her towel off when she reached the door. This time, I admired her toned physique with the full knowledge that this was my boss. Her voice faded as she entered the locker room. "Great, I'll look for your e-mail in a half-hour..."

When I rose from the small pool, I was hard. I did a quick check around the pool to make sure that it was still empty, then scampered to the locker room.

The showers were broken into individual stalls with plastic curtains. I could hear the water running on the other side of the wall. That didn't do anything to soften my erection. Separated by just a foot of painted cinder block, Linnea Sorenson was naked and very possibly covered in soap suds. I released a heavy sigh and stripped out of my damp trunks.

Just before my hand could cut on my own shower, I heard it—the unmistakable sound of female moaning. My ears strained, but I heard only the hiss of water on tile at first. Then it came again.

"Ahh..."

My cock bounced in my fist.

I looked around. The sound must be coming through the vents, set along the upper reaches of the wall. I briefly considered climbing up there to see if I could peer down before discarding that thought. Even I couldn't get that pervy. Still, the soft cries that reached my ears were pretty fucking good.

I sat on a bench in the handicap accessible stall and wrapped my hand around the chlorine coated sweep of my hard on. I pumped it slowly, surprised to feel the instant imminence of my orgasm. I bit my lip and furrowed my brow as Linnea's moans came quicker and louder. I shut my eyes, seeing her standing under the blur of the shower. In my mind, she reached one hand across her chest to clutch and pinch the opposite breast as the other worked between her thighs, two fingers curled inward as her thumb danced on her clit.

Linnea came in a soft hum. I followed right behind her, my arcing cum leaving a sticky mess all over my chest. I was glad I was in a shower.

As I recovered, I strained to hear her under the shower spray. Some heavy breathing. Something. She was still there. I could hear the way the water redirected as her body moved beneath it, but I got no more moans.

At last, the shower cut off. I waited ten long minutes before turning on my own shower and rinsing myself off.

I was still dazed after I was dressed. If someone would have told me a week ago that I would have heard the Director of Marketing masturbating—or that she did that at all—I would have thought it was absurd.

I was in my room no longer than five minutes when I heard a phone ring, although it took my three rings to realize it was *my* phone. 10:15. *Caller unknown.* I thought it might be Chuck, trying to get me back out, and feigned fatigue as I answered.

"Hello?"

Linnea Sorenson's voice greeted me like a sip of spiced wine. "I didn't wake you, did I?"

And like that, the fatigue, real or not, was gone. "No, no, I'm up. What's up?"

"Well, it's City Fitness. They're waffling."

Ah, now that phone call I'd overheard made sense. That was City Fitness.

"They like *zhu zhu*, but they want a few custom options added before they sign on."

"What are the options?"

You know when you ask someone's name, and then promptly stop listening? That's what happened here. I asked a question when I was incapable of processing the answer. My head was back in the locker room and my ears were filled with Linnea's muffled cries.

That was, until there was a pause on the other end, as if she was expecting something from me. So I gave the response that felt right. "That shouldn't be a problem…" I had no idea what the problem was.

"That's what I was hoping to hear. I've reserved the business center. I'll meet you down there in fifteen."

"Wait, what?" What had I just agreed to?

"The business center is located on mezzanine. Your room key should be able to open it, but I'll be there to let you in tonight. Or are you changing your mind about being able to solve this problem?"

There was a definite sense of *you better fucking not be* in that statement. I almost considered saying it.

"Okay. The business center. Mezzanine. I'll need coffee." I rubbed my eyes, wishing I hadn't had so much to drink. "Lots of coffee."

****

Linnea met me at the entrance of the hotel's business center. She'd put on a long, loose sweater that hung off her shoulders, along with a pair of black leggings. Her hair was still wet, I noticed, making her look more like a coed than a high-powered exec—although her attitude was all business.

"Thanks for getting here so quickly. Coffee and sandwiches are on the way from the kitchen. Red Bull, too."

Following her in, my eyes drifted down her slight body. I'd always thought of her as tall, but without her heels on and the command of her business attire, she seemed much smaller. I wished that the sweater wasn't so long—would have been nice to see her ass once again in those tight leggings—but the fresh smell of soap and chlorine helped fill my mind with enough filthy imagery to satisfy me.

Not that there was any possibility of something happening between Linnea and me, but in a masochistic kind of way, I was looking forward to spending the entire night working hard next to the blonde Finn. I liked thinking of myself as her hero—the guy who saved the code and landed the big deal.

So it was a big shock when I walked into the business center and found Casey hammering away at her laptop.

"Hey there, sleepyhead."

Casey was back to being Casey. She'd traded in her party dress for her familiar, gray hoodie, put her hair back into its typical ponytail, and taken out her contacts. She still wore an inordinate amount of make-up, but I was happy for that. It reminded me how stunning she could be, and that I shouldn't underestimate a thing about her.

She had one knee pulled up under her chin as she watched her computer compile something, and in that split second, I thought I caught a glimpse of a deeper beauty than what I'd seen out on the dance floor. Then she just became Casey.

"Okay, you two, let me explain what needs to be done…"

Linnea stayed with us for another hour, long enough for us to work through our initial solutions and ask questions when those didn't quite solve it. At first, both Casey and I figured we could get out of there shortly after she left, then things began to unravel.

"Jesus fuck," Casey said, stepping away from her computer with disgust.

"I don't think he did."

She pulled her glasses off, rubbed her eyes, and cracked another can of Red Bull. "Says you."

I got up from my station, stretching. My muscles were not happy with me. I longed for the Jacuzzi again—and that in turn reminded me of Linnea doing her laps…and more. I almost told Casey. Usually, when we got stuck on some code, the best thing to do was talk about anything but the problem.

Casey spoke first.

"So what happened tonight?"

At first, my mind couldn't get past that pool and locker room encounter. "What?"

"With you and that blonde. You just left without telling anyone. What did that bitch say to you?"

I blinked. Right. A whole lot of shit went down even before the pool. And it all came back to me in a flood. Dancing with Avery. My confusion. The unfinished drink in my hand.

"No, not that. I was just tired."

"The party animal Adam? Tired? I didn't think it was possible."

I didn't want to talk about this, so I changed the subject. "You clean up well, Case. I didn't even know you owned a dress."

"Well now you do. I'd wear it to work, but they tell me it's against the dress code."

I laughed. "Also, no one would be able to get any work done."

Casey smiled with me, but her expression turned introspective. "It's hard in this field. To be a woman, I mean. It's so male dominated that it's hard to be taken seriously."

"I take you seriously. You're an amazing coder."

"*Now* you say. But do you know how much I have to work to downplay my…femininity?" She squinted. "Is that a word?"

"I think so."

"It wasn't so bad in school. At least there, we were all competing for grades. Things were even. Out here, in the workforce, it's all fucked up." She sighed. "You're a good guy. Most guys aren't. In places I worked before, all they saw were a pair of tits. I'm not sure anyone even looked at my work. Do you know how hard it is to feel motivated when you're not appreciated?"

"I actually have no idea."

"Of course you don't."

"But I do appreciate you?" I offered.

Casey smiled tightly and plopped herself before her computer again. I watched her, wondering if I should say more when she pulled off her hoodie. She wore a purple racerback tank top, one that didn't hide the black straps of her bra or those distracting breasts.

I forced my attention away from the tanned plunge of her cleavage, over to the screen.

"Remember the work you did on the infrastructure piece last February?" I asked.

"Of course. It was awesome." Then, she got where I was going. "Why didn't I think of that?"

"Because you're just a pair of tits and a pretty smile?"

"Watch it, buddy, or I'm going to take back that thing I said about you being a good guy."

****

We finished up sometime around five in the morning. The cans of Red Bull filled the small recycling bin, and we'd switched from the somewhat healthy sandwiches that Linnea had sent down to pizza and chicken wings—essential fuel for the programmer.

I'm not sure how I stayed awake through the presentation. I grabbed a catnap that would have turned into something much longer were it not for the harsh wake-up call I'd set. The shower helped, too, although I was so out of it that I didn't even think about what I'd heard the last time I'd taken a shower.

Linnea and Casey were already there when I arrived, both managing to look like they'd received a full night's rest. My quasi-boss commanded most of my attention with her power suit—particularly because it was a dress, not her usual trousers and a blouse. Black, snug without being tight, and just short enough to boast long, shapely legs, Linnea wore a short white blazer over it to give it an added air of professionalism.

"Look who just dragged himself in," she said. "You're right, no tie."

Casey, next to her, grinned. "I don't think he owns one."

"I do. Should I go get it?"

I'd put on a pair of khakis and a blue Oxford that was relatively unwrinkled (thank God for no-iron shirts), but suddenly felt dressed down.

"No time," Linnea said. "It's fine. You have a nice *help desk* look going on there."

I looked at Casey, who was covering her smile. She'd cleaned up, too. The gray skirt was longer than Linnea's dress, but paired with a matching blazer, a crisp white blouse, and even a little belt around her waist, she actually looked like...well, like someone about to make a presentation before a major client.

She also looked hot, in a Linnea Sorenson understudy kind of way.

"Where did you get that?"

"Oh, this old thing?" She did a quick pirouette. "Actually, Linn helped me pick it out this morning when I realized my only dress was the one I wore last night."

A reminder of the tight sheath with its spangled top brought back a lot more memories of last night. I shoved them all away. "You should have worn that. We would have landed this contract before we even opened our mouths."

"See? No integrity," Casey said to Linnea.

The Finn looked at me. "No, he understands it more than you realize. When it comes to business, use every strength you've got. You're gorgeous, Case. Don't hide it."

I thought about what Casey had said last night and saw the bullish protest build in her face. Linnea went on, this time to me.

"We flirt with the line, but never cross it. The potential client should always be left wanting more, but should always respect you."

If that line of thinking was meant to describe her outfit, she nailed it. Everything about this woman was carefully crafted. The dress, the blazer, every blonde hair tucked into its neat coif, was there to do just what she'd said: to tease, to tantalize and promise, but to demand respect.

The image of bending her over the conference table, hiking up her dress, and taking her until she screamed came so suddenly that I actually gasped.

"Isn't that right, Adam?"

Linnea looked at me like she knew precisely what I was thinking about. How did she do that?

She controlled the presentation with the City Fitness folks just as she'd promised. It was a case study in how to market a product she knew nothing about. Linnea could have sold these guys a box of broken beer bottles and they would have gone for it happily. When they asked a question she didn't know how to answer, she turned to us—but these questions were rare. She spoke with more knowledge of our software than I'd thought she had, but did so without the technical jargon that Casey or I would have thrown in. They were riveted.

This was why she was a director and I was a worker bee. Like the outfit and her poise, Casey and I were props. We were there to demonstrate that she meant business—*go with us, and this is the kind of expertise you'll have on hand.*

"Well…" Tyler Kline, who seemed to be the man calling the shots, leaned back and surveyed the three of us. I felt my heart skip as we waited for his decision. "It's going to be fun working with you guys. Where do we sign?"

Casey and I visibly released our breath. If Linnea had been holding hers, she didn't show it.

She just smiled, stepped forward, and took his hand. "I've got the paperwork in my bag. And Mr. Kline, I'm not sure who's going to love this product more: you or your customers."

When he stood and took her hand, a flash of jealousy shot through me, as silly as that was. He was a good looking man in a blonde, American farmland kind of way.

"Call me Tyler. And I think I know who will be the most pleased." His eyes crinkled when he smiled in a way that had me hating him. He didn't release his hand. "Our bosses are going to love both of us for this deal."

Linnea gracefully stepped away, although the smiles she was sharing with Tyler bothered me. I was the one who was supposed to melt the Director of Ice, not some square-jawed stranger.

"I think you're right."

She walked over to her attaché case and pulled out a folder. "No need to sign now. Take your time, look them over—have your lawyers look them over, too—and send them back to our offices."

Tyler didn't even look at the folder. His eyes never left my boss. "Will do."

The other two guys beside him started to pack up. Casey shut down our laptop and started to do the same. I just stood there, feeling unhelpful and fine with that.

"I'd like to invite you to a reception City Fitness is sponsoring tomorrow night. It's a networking thing for other gyms, but…" He waved the folder in front of him. "…I think this makes us partners now, don't you?"

My jealousy hit a new high.

"We'd love to join you," she said at last, looking at Casey and me.

If Tyler was put off by our inclusion, it didn't register in his face. He simply turned his thousand-watt smile on us and nodded. "Great. I'll make sure that your names are added to the list." He smacked the folder. "And I'll have this over to your offices by the end of the day. Wouldn't want you peddling this little gem to our competition."

"Wouldn't dream of it," Linnea said. "I always leave with the one I came in with."

Tyler grinned, thanked us again, and was gone.

And that's when Linnea finally released her breath and slumped against the conference table. She looked up at the ceiling and laughed. "We did it."

"That was awesome, Linn," Casey said.

"Impressive," I agreed, although begrudgingly.

"Thank you, you two." She came over and hugged us. I could smell the chlorine on her beneath her perfume and my mind went to dirty places. "You just made us a ton of money."

"You handled that sales guy really well," Casey said. "You practically had him eating out of your hand."

"It helps when they look as good as he did," Linnea said.

I had no right to feel jealous, but I did.

Casey giggled. "He was pretty hot, wasn't he? If you pass on him, maybe I'll see if he wants to test drive our equipment tomorrow night."

Linnea actually laughed out loud. "Once we have that contract signed, you can do whatever you want. I'm not going to judge."

"I'm starting to feel a little jealous." There was a lot more truth to my statement than the joke let on.

"Don't worry, Adam," Casey said. "Linn and I already spent all morning talking about you."

I looked at Linnea, then back to Casey, but couldn't tell if they were fucking with me or not. I was too tired to think.

I shouldered my bag. "I'm going to grab some sleep. I feel like the walking dead here."

Linnea nodded. "You earned it. You did great."

"I just stood there and smiled."

"Like I said, you did great."

Linnea and Casey laughed again.

"Okay, I'm out of here. See you tonight."

"Tonight?" my boss asked.

"You're going to buy me a drink." I was too tired to worry about what I was saying.

"Is that right?"

"It is. Eight o'clock in the hotel's rooftop bar."

There was challenge in her eyes, but not in her reply. "Go get some sleep, Adam. I'll see you later."

chapter two

I had no idea whether she'd be there. Part of me hoped that she wouldn't. She challenged me in ways that I wasn't used to. It actually took effort to converse with her, unlike girls like Brooke or Avery. Also, there was no possibility of getting laid.

That was my biggest realization after waking from my nap. I was horny. For the first time since last night, I thought I might regret turning down the advances of the sexy yogi. She wasn't Linnea—or *Linn*, as Casey kept calling her—but would have provided a release, and as awful as that sounded, that was what I needed.

Maybe I could go out after tonight's drink and find someone. I had Chuck's number, and he was definitely going out.

But first, I had a date with Linnea Sorenson. It was stupid but as I showered, shaved, and prepared, I started to treat it like a date. I got nervous. I took too long deciding on a slim pair of jeans and a crisp button-down—even ironed it this time. I checked myself out in the mirror, happy with the way the dark chocolate shirt emphasized my broad shoulders and dark hair. I wondered if cologne would be too much, then said *fuck it* and sprayed some on anyway.

Linn was an executive. She was my superior. She was at least fifteen years older than me. And the kicker: she was married. She was already someone else's and as morally flexible as I was, that was a line I'd never crossed. So I knew that it was far-fetched to even dream of something happening, but I dreamed it anyway. All it took was a recollection of the older woman in that workout bikini and I was hooked.

My heart was all over the place as I stepped off the elevators. When I walked into the bar, a trendy place that was located on the top floor of our hotel, I had to laugh at myself. I'd imagined this evening as a one-on-one, Linn and myself, but it seemed that the whole team was there, crowded around a table and laughing boisterously.

Linn was standing in their midst, which was a little incongruous for her, but not really that strange. It looked like a work happy hour and she was the token exec, there to pick up the check. What it certainly wasn't was an intimate drink with a potential lover. I felt like an idiot. That thought was definitely going to be a secret that I would take to my grave. I shook my head and picked my way through the crowd.

"The hero is finally awake," Chuck said, raising his beer bottle at me. "What're you drinking?"

I looked at Linnea, who was quietly sipping at a martini glass filled with something pale green. She saluted me as I settled in beside Chuck.

"I'll take a bourbon and Coke," I said.

After the night and crazy morning, I couldn't help but feel like these people were imposing. So much had happened since last I'd seen them.

"Good thing you struck out with Avery." To Linnea: "That would have been an awkward call."

Chuck was drunk. Judging from the amused expression Linnea

wore, I didn't think he normally spoke to her like that.

"I wouldn't say *awkward*," she said. "Maybe frustrating for Adam, but I've found that sometimes that energy can be put to good use."

"You've found, huh?" I asked. My bourbon and Coke arrived.

"A little denial can be a healthy thing." Her eyes flashed, hazel and mesmerizing.

Chuck came crashing in. "Well, neither Brooke nor Avery denied me last night. They didn't deny each other, either."

I groaned, feeling a little embarrassed for the guy. Was he like this last night, only I'd been too drunk to notice? "How long have you guys been here?"

"Since we got off!" Casey cheered loudly, joining the group from wherever she'd been. "But Linn here just joined us."

The shift would have ended at 6, which meant two hours of happy hour drinking.

"I had some things to take care of...like confirming that City Fitness is in!"

"So it's official." Chuck wore a smug smile, as though he'd done anything. Casey actually hugged Linnea with a squeal she wouldn't have dreamed of giving were she sober.

"I'll drink to that," I said, and downed most of my Jack and Coke. I needed to catch up, after all.

The group fell apart about a drink or so later when Chuck suggested they move the party to a strip club and the booth crew—including Casey, surprisingly—all agreed with enthusiasm.

Linn bowed out, but then again it would have been surprising if she'd gone. As for me, I suddenly saw the opportunity to hang out with the pretty blonde and had enough to drink that that seemed like a better option than strippers.

"I think I'll stay back and finish my drink, but thanks," I said.

"Text me where you're at and maybe I'll meet up with you."

"Suit yourself."

As Linn moved to pick up her purse and join the exodus, I stopped her with a smile. "You still owe me a drink, Linnea Sorenson."

She cocked her head. "What'll it be, Adam Murphy?"

I'd been drinking whiskey and Cokes, but I figured I should step it up. Wasn't every day I got to drink on a director's dime. "I'll take a bourbon on the rocks. You pick."

I turned to attend to the men's room, my order feeling like a victory.

Linnea was sitting alone on a barstool when I returned, two amber glasses sitting in front of her. She was still wearing her outfit from this morning's meeting, although the white blazer was gone. She had nice arms, toned and unblemished, and I spotted the hint of black bra strap at the shoulders.

I took a deep breath for courage, crossed the room, and sat with purpose. Picking up my drink, I made a toast. "So, here's to making loads of money."

Linn laughed. It did this electric, zippy thing up my spine. "Let's try, *to teamwork,* instead."

"Doesn't have quite the same ring to it, but sure. Teamwork wins." I sipped, a little surprised when the bourbon didn't immediately scald my throat. "Wow, this is smooth. What is it?"

"Woodford Reserve. It's one of my favorites."

I nodded, pretending to agree when, in fact, I had never heard of the brand. Linn took another sip, savoring the smoky spirit.

"Mmm, that's good," she said.

"Well, thanks."

I wondered where all my courage went as we sat quietly, sipping at our drinks without much to say. I didn't know much about her, I realized, and talking shop was the last thing I wanted to do after staying up all night working on it.

It was Linnea who broke the ice.

"Tell me something interesting."

I could have said anything. *Something interesting* was a pretty broad topic, but my mind was still snagged on last night in the pool and locker room. I couldn't get away from it, and the bourbon was strong enough that I couldn't stop the next thing from slipping out.

"I heard the most interesting thing last night."

"Do tell."

"It was late. 9:45 or so, and I was just finishing up a soak in the hotel's hot tub." I looked up at her. I'd been so preoccupied with the rest of her that I'd never noticed how gorgeous her hazel eyes were—like a mountain lion's. They were all I could look at, and when I did, I didn't see the embarrassment I was expecting.

"The one on the 30th floor? I bet that was nice. They have a nice pool facility here."

I had tried to get her off balance, and now it was me who was stumbling and uncertain. But like the drunken fool that I could be, I went on. "Their showers are pretty relaxing, too. The perfect place to let off some steam."

"I agree."

Don't blush. Don't blush. "Can I get you another drink?"

"Order *yourself* one," she said. "You look like you need it."

Linn was different than anyone else I'd flirted with. I thought of Brooke from last night and how the flirting was just a formality to the one-night stand. With Linn, the banter was challenging, and a hell of a lot more fun.

I ordered the two of us another round of the same, feeling squeezed by the expense even though I wasn't paying for it. Linnea didn't bat an eyelash.

I said, "So what about you? Why don't you tell me something interesting."

She caressed the rim of her glass as she thought, her eyes far away. When they swung back to me, my cock stiffened. She could look at me like that forever.

"When I get stressed, I get horny." Her gaze never left mine.

My response caught in my throat. "And last night, you were stressed?"

"The deal of the decade was slipping away. You could say I was a little stressed."

"You could have called me."

"I thought I did, didn't I? And you did save me."

"I mean about the...stressed thing."

Not even a blush, although she did look away and smile. I took the opportunity to check her out. Her dress was tight enough that I could see the tiny bumps of her hardening nipples high on her swells. "I can take care of myself."

"So I heard."

We shared the space in silence, neither of us wanting to rush from this moment. I smiled. She smiled. We enjoyed being here. When Linnea spoke, she decided to take things to the next level.

"So how was the pool's hot tub?"

"Relaxing." I had a hunch where she was going and took a chance. "In fact, I'm thinking of heading there after this drink."

"I'll join you. After the day I had, I could go for some relaxing." She pushed away from the bar, where she'd been leaning. "In fact, why wait to finish these? Pool's only one floor down. Let's take them with us."

It felt like someone very large and very strong had come up behind me, wrapped his arms around my chest, and squeezed. Somehow, I managed to nod and smile. "Lead the way."

****

We took the elevators down one level without even a consideration to detouring to our rooms. I wasn't sure about Linnea, but I didn't have a suit in the locker room. I didn't say a thing. I was along for the ride.

This time, the doors to the pool room were closed and the lights off. I was buzzing, and it was from more than just the drinks I'd consumed. Sneaking into a pool at night felt inherently electrifying. Doing it with your married boss, intentions unknown, cranked the wattage up one hundred times.

"The facilities are closed after nine, but..." Linnea passed her key-card along the lock and the light went from red to green. "I called in a few favors. I can't make it to the pool during the day, and I'm not going to miss out on my laps. Even for business."

I followed her in, the smell of chlorine and rubber greeting us. She didn't turn on any lights, and made sure to close the door behind her. "This is what I should have done last night."

"I'm glad you didn't," I said with about as much confidence as I could muster. My heart was trying to climb up my throat and I didn't trust myself to say any more.

We passed the front desk, piled neatly with white towels. Linnea handed me one, then took another for herself. Then we arrived at the doors to the locker rooms—the crossroads where business met pleasure. I looked at the female sign on the door down Linnea's path: the white outline in the dress and a pair of chunky legs. I couldn't think of a more inappropriate symbol to mark what happened behind those doors.

"I'll meet you out there." Linnea offered me one last teasing smile, then pushed through the door and was gone.

I went into my own locker room before I realized I had no idea what I was supposed to do. Strip down to my underwear? Go naked? Should I play it safe and go straight through, fully clothed, and see what Linnea did on the other side?

I immediately crossed that last one off the list. It's what my blonde boss wanted: to keep me always following her lead. This was a power game as surely as any other, and I wasn't going to let her win so easily.

Thing was, the more I thought about it, the more I realized how low my odds were. I pulled my shirt over my head, catching my reflection in the mirror as I worked through the possibilities. If I went out there in my boxer-briefs and Linnea was soaking naked, then I'd appear bashful. If I went out there naked and Linnea wasn't, then I'd be brash and uncouth. I'd have to guess, and I still didn't have a handle on Linnea Sorenson.

Chances of her soaking in roiling water naked were low. So was she leading me on? She'd asked to join me and knew that I knew about her fun in the shower last night. So was that an invitation for more?

Bah! I kicked out of my shoes and socks, shoved my jeans down to my ankles, and took a look at myself again. My black boxer-briefs molded around the sizable lump of my cock, and as I imagined Linnea's eyes darting there as I walked up to her, it started to grow.

She was European. Maybe the rules of propriety were different for her? I knew a little about Finnish culture and their love of saunas: lounge naked, jump into cold water to cool off, then back to the sauna. And if I remembered correctly, that was all done naked. Was a hot tub a different beast?

"Fuck it," I said, then dropped my underwear and grabbed the towel. If I was going to lose this game, I was going to do it boldly.

My cock swelled and swung between my legs, but didn't get hard enough to begin standing up. That was good. Walking out there with a full-on erection would have been a hell of a lot harder to do.

My glass of bourbon resting against my hip, my shoulders back, and my chest puffed out, I pushed out into the pool proper. This was no different than walking through a crowded gym locker to the showers; I just needed to put one foot in front of the other and don't think about the nudity.

Linnea was already in the Jacuzzi, submerged to her neck. She'd twisted her blonde hair into a messy bun on top of her head and wore a smile the whole time. When she looked down at my cock, the smile grew wider.

My erection started to strengthen, and it took every ounce of will-power to keep my casual stride and not to run for the water.

"Just letting it all hang out, I see," she said, rising enough out of the water that I could see her black bra straps on her shoulders. *Shit*.

"It's not often I get to hot tub in private. I thought I'd take advantage."

I reached the edge of the pool, stepped up, and slid in. The hot water felt good as it slithered around my thighs and caressed my cock. Best of all, though, it covered my nudity.

"Well, thanks for that. It was a nice show." She reached for her glass of bourbon. It was almost empty. "You have a nice body, Adam."

With the water pressing down around me, my confidence began to recharge. "Thank you. I'd say the same, but I didn't get a chance to see yours."

"Oh, you don't want to see an old woman like me naked." Judging from that smirk, I knew she didn't really believe her words. "I bet you get a lot of attention from the girls."

"I do alright."

"Guys who shave their cock and balls don't do just *alright*."

I blinked.

"I like it, by the way. I've never seen one like that, but it's a nice look."

"Thanks." Fuck, that was a lame answer.

"So what happened last night? Casey said you left alone."

I thought of Casey and how she'd come on to me.

"You didn't leave because of me, did you?"

"I..." I wasn't going to tell her the truth, was I? "You think very highly of yourself, don't you?"

Linnea's smile was languid. "I do. And you didn't answer my question."

"I left because I was tired."

"Tired enough to come down here and spy on me?"

"I didn't know you were down here." Okay, that sounded defensive. "And I couldn't sleep."

"Hmm...something's not adding up, Adam."

She lifted the glass of bourbon to her mouth, her diamond ring catching in the light. I seized that, trying to regain my balance. "Does it even matter? What would your husband think about you in a hot tub with a naked guy?"

As soon as the words left my mouth, I realized any prospect I had of sleeping with her was gone. Reminding her of her moral obligations wasn't the best way to seduce a woman.

"My husband would probably love to know." I just looked at her, confused, so she explained. "Our relationship is...complicated. He has this fantasy involving me and other men." The revelation washed over me without sinking in. "He'd probably wish that I was naked, too."

That makes two of us, I thought, but just couldn't manage to say.

I had no clue what the fuck was going on, but my cock had a

pretty good idea and was now standing at full length beneath the turbulent water.

"Show me," she said.

We'd been walking the fine line of decorum. Flirting up in the bar was dubious enough. Sharing a private hot tub soak was questionable. Telling me to show her my erect cock? Nothing borderline about that. It was sexual harassment, almost by definition. I met her challenging stare. There was nothing apologetic in that gaze.

So what did I do? I hoisted myself up onto the edge of the Jacuzzi and felt her eyes slide all over me.

I knew I looked good. My muscles stood out, clearly defined as water glistened off my skin. When Linn's eyes walked down my torso, I flexed the six-pack I worked so hard to maintain, getting a smile of appreciation for my efforts.

Then her eyes arrived at my cock, standing at its full eight, impressive inches.

"Someone's excited. That's not because of me, is it?"

The cat was playing with the mouse.

"You know what they call me at work, right? *The Director of Ice.* I know all about it. Remember, I control message and brand. Who do you think first circulated that nickname?" She finally took her eyes off my cock. "Do you think of me as...chilly?"

She already knew the answer to that, so I didn't bother answering it. "Your husband's fantasy...have you ever acted on it?"

She stared at me for the longest time. "Not yet."

Linnea's face was filled with glittering promise. It made my cock flex and bounce between my legs. Linnea caught it, those hazel eyes sliding down to watch it again. She licked her lips.

"At first, I thought it was because he wanted to be with someone else. Another woman. I got pretty jealous of that. But he swore up and down that it wasn't that. He couldn't really explain it. It just turned him on."

She waded into the middle of Jacuzzi, her shoulders once again disappearing beneath the roiling water.

"Took me a long time to come to grips with that, and when I realized he wasn't trying to orchestrate some kind of swapping, swinging thing, I started fantasizing about it, too...although I never told him. I told myself if I was going to do this, it was going to be for me, not to fulfill his fantasy."

She fiddled with something beneath the water, and suddenly she was tossing her sodden bra up beside me.

"Has anyone told you that you've got control issues?" I asked.

"I like being in control. Why would that be an issue?"

Linnea closed the gap between us. When she rose from the water enough to wrap her hand around the base of my cock and look up at me with those mountain lion eyes, any answer was lost.

"Tell me, Adam, am I about to fulfill *your* fantasy?"

I couldn't even answer *that* question intelligently. I didn't have to. Linn dropped her head and took me into her mouth.

My balls seized. My breath caught. I came as close to losing it as possible without actually losing it. Stars burst behind my eyelids as I squeezed them shut and fought back from the brink.

Linn eased off my shaft, her soft lips fastened around it the whole way. When I popped free, she held it to the side and looked up at me. "Did you ever think the Director of Ice would suck your cock?" She kissed along the sensitive underside, dipping lower. "Or suck your balls?"

I groaned, leaning back into my arms as she swallowed my scrotum into her mouth. Her tongue swirled around my testicles, short-circuiting my brain.

"I love how smooth they are. I'm going to have to get Mark to start shaving himself."

She didn't give me a chance to say a word before she returned to sucking my balls, this time with the addition of a slow hand job. I wasn't going to last much longer, no matter how strong my willpower was. She was good. She was also my fucking boss!

Linnea sensed my imminence, too, and pulled away again. She continued to stroke me with her hand, ever so slowly, just to keep me on the edge.

"That feel good?"

I nodded. She seemed to like that I couldn't speak.

"Tell me truthfully, Adam. Last night, you had your pick of the club. You're hot. You're confident. And this is Vegas. Hook-ups are easier here. I bet you could have fucked Casey if you wanted to."

My cock reacted at the thought of the busty brunette. Linnea felt it, too, but didn't say anything.

"So why didn't you? Was it because you were thinking about me?"

I couldn't lie any longer. Not in this position, and not this addled by sex. "Yes. I couldn't stop thinking about you. And...no one could compare to you."

Linnea's smile lit up her beautiful face. "Thanks for being honest."

In reward, she shifted up, wrapped her lips around my cock, and started blowing me. And Jesus Christ, did she feel good. She sucked, she swirled, she bobbed along my length like nothing I'd felt before.

The pressure built with each stroke. She squeezed the base of my cock with both hands, rising further from the water as she angled into me. I caught the flash of nipple, pale pink and swollen. I wanted to see more of her body. Knew that I would. Knew that soon, I'd see her lithe frame dancing over me.

I reached down with one hand, lacing my fingers through her wet hair. *Yes, just like that, just like that...* This was my dream: to feel the Ice Director melt all over my cock. She wanted control, but couldn't control herself when it came to me. My balls tightened. I was seconds away. Seconds away from exploding inside Linnea Sorenson's hot mouth. Seconds away from this hot wife drinking my cum because she couldn't help herself.

Five. Four. Three. Two—

Linnea yanked her mouth off and sank back beneath the water just before I exploded. "Well that was fun, but I'm burning up. Aren't you?"

I was a soap bubble, poised to pop at even the most gentle of breezes. Yet Linnea denied even that. Turning away from me, she rose out of the hot tub, water cascading around her near-naked body. A black thong bisected the ass I'd admired on the plane, as perfect naked as I'd imagined. But even that image didn't get me over the hump.

"I'm headed up to bed. I've got a long day tomorrow, and then there's the party at night. I'll see you then?"

"I thought..."

"You thought that you were in control. Now you know you're not."

She circled the hot tub wide, giving me a glimpse of her tits, but not the full show. They sat small and high, well-formed for her slender body.

"Have a good night, Adam."

When she was gone, I flopped onto my back, my feet still in the swirling water, and groaned.

chapter three

Sleep was just not something I was going to get. Not for a while.

I slid back into the hot tub, letting the jets settle my ragged heart-beat. Linnea Sorenson, paragon of professionalism, had just given me a blowjob in the public pool. How the fuck was I supposed to just crawl into bed and get some shut eye?

I considered joining the rest of the team out at the strip club. I had the name waiting for me on my cellphone, along with a photo of a blonde stripper wearing a glittery bikini giving a laughing Casey a lapdance. But I'd already been playing catch-up when I joined them earlier. Judging from that photo, they were so far gone that I'd have to mainline whiskey, and I just wasn't in the mood.

Instead, I hit the casinos, settling down at a poker table that eventually drained my money around 4 in the morning as I turned over Linn's parting statement of the night: *You thought you were in control...*

Did I? Yeah, I probably did. I could have left with anyone at the club that first night; she'd been right about that. Did I go home alone because part of me decided to save myself for Linn?

I still wasn't convinced. Even now, after what had just happened, she seemed so unattainable. Tomorrow, she was holding a workshop before a few hundred people on the value of guerilla marketing. I'm not sure I could even define what that meant.

If I thought I'd been in control, however, I knew now that I wasn't. She'd demonstrated that with crystal clarity, and I had a pair of sore balls and a fast-fading memory to back it up.

I didn't get much sleep that night, but neither did my coworkers. And *my* late night didn't come with a hangover (or very much of one). When I rejoined the team that morning, Casey looked like a frayed version of her normal self. Her ponytail was looser. Her eyes were red behind her dark-framed glasses. Her normally perfect posture was slumped and tired.

"You look like you had some fun last night," I said as I came to relieve her.

She shut her eyes and held up her hand. "Please don't yell."

I chuckled. "Was that lapdance as fun as it looked?"

Casey groaned. "I will never. Have another. Tequila shot. Again."

"Until we go out tonight?"

Chuck joined us, looking no better off than Casey. He hadn't even bothered to tuck his polo into his khakis.

"Casey here ended up having a great time with that stripper. Didn't you, Case?"

My ears perked up. My groin stirred. "Yeah?"

"It was the tequila shots," she said flatly.

"We all ended up in the private dance area, although Casey got the most attention. I can tell you that while there's no sex in the champagne room, there's definitely a lot of girl-on-girl making out."

I shot a look at Casey, now wishing I *had* met them after all. "Wow."

Casey blushed something furious. "Tequila makes me do crazy things. I'm not usually into that sort of thing."

"Strippers? Or girls."

"Both?" She looked around the room. "I'm going to take a nap. I'll see you guys at the reception thing tonight?"

"See you then." Chuck seemed to draw energy from the exchange, but when she was gone, he slumped back into his hungover self. "Dude, I'm gassed."

"We're only halfway through the week. Ever thought of pacing yourself?"

Chuck screwed up his face. "This is Vegas. Why would I do that?"

Fair enough. It was something I thought I'd be saying around this point. Party hard and be happy to pay for it in the morning, right? Where had that version of Adam gone?

"I don't know, man, but you're totally right."

****

The shift crawled. Part of that was from not getting enough sleep. Part of it was that once the lunch hour rush was over, the convention hall died. Chuck left early. I killed time flirting with the girls in the yoga booth—part of me hoping that Linnea would come by and get jealous.

She didn't show up, but the guy from City Fitness did.

"Adam right?" he asked, his handshake firm. "Tyler Kline. Excellent work yesterday. You guys do a hell of a job."

"Thanks." It was nice to hear praise directly from the source—something that we coders didn't get much of—but something about this guy just rubbed me the wrong way.

"It's been nice working with Linn, too." I got his meaning. He didn't need to pistol-wink and cock his head to let me know that was a guy-to-guy comment. I felt immediately protective, even though I had no right. "That other developer, too. Casey? How do you get any work done with all these good looking women around?"

I forced a laugh—sounded pretty genuine, too. "It's a tough job, but someone's got to do it."

"It's either a fantasy come true, or hell each day," he said.

I thought about last night. Definitely a little of both.

"Well, I haven't actually worked with Linn much, but she's extremely professional around us. She's the kind of person who doesn't even have pictures of her family in her office, you know?"

She's got a family, asshole, so stay away, is what I really wanted to say, as hypocritical as that was.

"I do. I know the type very well." I didn't like that wolfish grin, or the implication. "Can't wait to see you guys tonight. It'll be fun. Just be ready to let loose. I know I will."

"Later."

Tyler was fit—as any purchaser for a gym chain should be. It pained me to admit it, but if Linn really wanted to fulfill her husband's fantasy (and her own), that guy was a better candidate than me. He wore no ring, was closer to her age, and was from her world: the one that lived on airplanes and in hotel rooms. The set-up could be perfect.

There was the snag where he was now a client, but the contract was already signed. Linnea herself had told Casey that she could do whatever she wanted once the ink was dry. Well, the ink was fucking dry.

My exhaustion hit me as I packed away our collaterals and closed up the booth. My brain shut down as soon as my head hit the pillow. When I woke up, it was dark. For one, quick moment, I panicked. Had I slept through the night? The reception?

My dreams fled, although I think I'd been dreaming about the hot tub again, only it wasn't me in there with Linnea, but Tyler. And Tyler wasn't denied the way I was.

Sitting up in bed, I realized I'd sweated through my clothes. Checking the clock, it was only 9. I'd missed an hour of it—and my grumbling stomach reminded me that I'd missed dinner, too—but I could still make it.

I splashed water on my face, trying to wash away my grogginess. On top of the jet lag, I'd stayed up all night two days ago, slept all day, had too much to drink the night before, and then decided to stay up until four a.m.

This required a shower to wash away, and when I stepped beneath the hot spray, I wondered if I shouldn't just stay here for the rest of the evening. At least here, I was in total control. I thought about Linnea, rising from the pool, naked and wet. She looked over her shoulder at me, promise in her eyes and the upturn of her lips.

I soaped my cock and balls, slithering my hands around the smooth skin. Behind closed eyes, it was Linnea's hands on my manhood. She knelt on the floor, looking up at me with those wild, hazel eyes.

Did you ever think the Director of Ice would suck your cock?

When the fantasy director did, I nearly came. I gasped, staring up at the ceiling as the imagery danced out of my head. No. This is what she wanted. For me to jack off thinking about her, and even if she never knew, I wasn't giving her the pleasure.

Instead, I grabbed my razor and shaved myself smooth. Tonight, someone was going to experience this—my blonde boss was number one on the list, but if she kept insisting on control, I was prepared to show her I didn't take a leash well.

****

The reception was a much bigger deal than I'd expected. I'd imagined a small gathering in someone's suite with passed *hors d'oeuvres* and someone's iPod playing music over portable speakers. When I read the invitation and realized it was actually in one of the ballrooms in the neighboring casino, I had to hurry so as not to lose more time.

By the time I made it down there, things had already begun to deteriorate. I could feel the low reverberation of the drums and bass guitar from down the hall, even with the doors shut.

"Do you have your name tag, sir?"

I didn't see the usher until I was standing in front of the double doors, reaching for entrance. "Name tag?"

She held up her own, tucked into a plastic sleeve and hanging from a lanyard. "We need to scan you, to make sure you're on the list."

"Oh right, sorry." I pulled it from the inside of my jacket.

"Are you okay, honey?" She had a sweet, motherly look to her. Her concern was genuine.

"I'm fine. Why?"

"You just look nervous. That's all."

"I'm fine."

"Well, have fun with your friends."

She opened the door. The wall of sound struck me in the gut before my eyes could adjust. I saw only shapes: silhouettes dancing on a lighted stage; eight-foot rounds making a wasteland in the darkness, covered in forgotten wine glasses and half-eaten meals. Throngs massed around the bar stations. A rock band thrashed on the stage.

So many people, I despaired, searching for *my* people on the dance floor or at the bars. Everyone was dressed in their evening's finest—suits, little cocktail dresses, glittering jewelry. I felt dressed down in my black suit, like I'd just walked in off the street.

I found Chuck first, near one of the bars, naturally, along with one of the guys from City Fitness who wasn't Tyler. As I approached, the guy broke off and headed back onto the dance floor.

"You look like you're dressed for a funeral, pal," Chuck said. He glanced at my black skinny tie. It was the only tie I owned and had, in fact, purchased it for my grandmother's funeral. "Don't worry, we'll get you laid tonight."

"Thanks, but I don't need your help there. I guess I'm just pickier than you."

Chuck grinned, enjoying the banter. He looked off at something in the crowd.

"You know you have no chance, right? They don't call her the Director of Ice for nothing."

My face slipped for maybe a second. "What are you talking about?"

"Ha. I'm telling you, man, it's not going to happen. She doesn't play that game."

"You've tried?"

Chuck shrugged. "She's my boss, so not really, but *of course!* I mean, look at her."

I did, following his eyes. She stood on the opposite side of the room, talking with Tyler Kline. She wore a slender black dress that fastened up the side. Buttoned up, it would have been suitable for a board meeting. With three golden buttons undone at the bottom, like now, and plenty of toned thigh visible, it was perfect for a night like this.

Chuck kept on talking. "I don't blame you. She's hot. Worse, she's hot and smart, and knows how to use it. But we're in Vegas. I don't want you to squander it chasing the unattainable when there are so many other chicks out here ready for it."

Casey joined us at that moment.

"What are you two whispering about?"

"Case in point," Chuck said with a laugh.

There was nothing particularly racy about Casey's dress. It was tame compared to the majority of women in the room. But the short black halter dress that scooped up her impressive bust was a further reminder that she was an attractive woman, not just my nerdy coworker.

"Cat got your tongue, Adam?" Casey asked. I couldn't keep my eyes from drifting into that deep well of cleavage.

"Sorry, what?"

Casey laughed. "I thought you were going to lame out on us again. Glad you could make it."

"I'm sorry I'm not into strippers as much as you."

At least that got her to blush. She changed the subject.

"Looks like Linn might be headed for a night of fun."

"Really?" Why did that sound like a whine in my ears?

"He's been at it most of the evening, and he's pretty charming."

"But she's married." *Now look at you, up on your high horse.* "And she's too smart to fall for him."

Casey glanced at Chuck, who was smirking. Casey went on, lashing away, completely unaware of what this was doing to me. "Dude, she's not looking to fall in love. She's looking to get laid."

I looked at Chuck. "When she travels...has she ever...?"

Chuck shook his head. "We don't travel much, but this is the most I've ever seen her smile. Maybe Casey's right. I mean, like I said, she's a good looking woman, she knows it—"

"And she knows how to use it," Casey finished. "Also, Tyler's really hot."

I watched Linnea's body language through a field of green. I watched her eyes. She appeared to be hanging onto his every word. Was that real attraction? Or was she playing him? Last night, she'd told me that she'd never fulfilled her husband's fantasy, but she seemed poised to. Did it matter that it wasn't with me? I felt betrayed.

Linn put her empty wine glass down and followed Tyler. She was smiling at him. What I wouldn't give to be the one receiving that look. They headed for the dance floor, and I had to admit they looked good; they had that Arian beauty to them, blonde and lean and sculpted.

I turned back to the bar, ready to order another. Chuck was one step ahead, a drink for me ready already. "This'll help."

"It's fine. Whatever. So have either of you actually done any gambling here?"

"I've checked out all the casinos, but mostly to check out the cocktail waitresses. The Venetian's are the best so far, if you like legs..."

Chuck hadn't been lying, he'd done his research. As he went into the details, Casey rolled her eyes and wandered away. I half-listened, but couldn't stop glancing over and Tyler and Linn. Yeah, this is the guy who'd fulfill her fantasy. Not me. He was right for her. They even danced the same way—the way my parents danced at weddings when they knew people were watching.

When Tyler pulled her into his arms and whispered something into her ear—which she laughed off—I almost went over there and broke things up.

"So she's never acted like this?"

Chuck stopped whatever he was saying and followed my eyes. "Never. I can't really believe that woman's my boss, actually. She usually does a little flirting, but she's usually gone by now, too."

"Interesting."

Chuck slapped me on the back. "You still have no fucking chance."

As that idea sunk in, so did something more terrifying. What if our conversation last night woke something in Linn? She'd not only admitted her husband's cuckold fantasy, but had admitted that she was into the idea—on her own terms. I looked at Tyler. Was that her own terms?

She'd given me a fucking blowjob in the hot tub. Anything was possible.

One thing I knew was for sure: I needed to get away from the bar. Chuck, too, judging by the way he'd begun to slur his words.

We found Casey with the rest of our contingent. Everyone was beginning to look worn down, although they still talked like they were going to go out.

"And this is my wonderful team," Linn was saying as they got into earshot of us. "You met Adam and Casey at the meeting yesterday. I'd like you to meet Chuck, my right hand man."

Chuck sized Tyler up, shaking his hand firmly like he was either an overbearing father or a precocious younger brother. Either way, Tyler took that in stride.

"Nice to meet you, Chuck." To everyone: "I'm glad that everyone could make it. Linn talks very highly about you guys." He had a politician's smile, even white teeth and all.

While he exchanged small talk with Chuck and the sales team, I gave Linnea my attention. "You look good."

Up close, I realized just how true my statement was. Her hair was done in little blonde ringlets, two spirals framing her glossy face. With her hair down, she looked younger than however old she was, although no one my age could afford those sparkling, teardrop earrings.

"Thank you, Adam. You clean up well, too, although I'd recommend a more colorful tie." And like that, the perceived youth was gone and the executive was back.

"So how did your workshop go today?" I asked.

"Very well. Only had a handful of people walked out."

"Linn's being modest," Tyler said, joining our conversation like a cancer metastasizing. He even set his hand on the small of her back.

"She had the crowd riveted."

"Please, I'm not sure riveted was the right word."

"Trust me, I've been to a few workshops, and yours was one of the better ones."

"Just *one of the better ones*?"

"I have high standards," he said. He gave her a significant look.

Watching the exchange, I felt like an outsider. Jealousy churned in my gut. I wondered if I should leave them alone—make some excuse, like needing a refill. Then realized that that was the last thing I was going to do.

"So what are people's plans after the party?"

Linn and Tyler turned to me, as though remembering I was there. I caught Casey's smirk out of the corner of my eye.

"Well," Tyler answered, "I don't have much planned. Figured I'd keep my options open."

He didn't need to look at Linn for me to know what his number one option was. I glanced at my boss, who was studying me with a hint of amusement.

"A bunch of us are going dancing," Chuck said loudly. He was having trouble with volume control. "You in, guys?"

"I think I'm too old for that." Linn smiled, the amusement shifting to her drunk employee. "Chuck, maybe you should take a break. Or slow down, at least."

"I'm fine." There was a wino's clumsy inflection in his words. A moment later, he proved that he was most certainly not fine. "Excuse me. I need to—"

And then he bolted for the restroom.

Tyler laughed. Linn looked at me, halfway between amused and concerned. She gestured towards the bathroom with her chin. *Follow him.*

I did.

Chuck was hugging the toilet bowl when I got to him. I thought of snapping a picture of it: the brash young marketer on his hands and knees in a crisp gray suit, his tie smeared with vomit. I decided to give him his dignity and began running paper towels under the faucet.

"One day, you better do this shit for me," I grunted as I yanked off his tie.

"I didn't have that much to drink," he slurred.

"Maybe you got a bad batch of...what were you drinking?"

After a pause: "I don't remember."

"Well, then it's time for you to go back to your room. Come on, up you go."

I led him out into the main room, where the party kept on going without us. Tyler, Linn, and Casey were still chatting, although the rest of the team had dispersed.

"You feel better, Chuck?" Linn asked.

"He's done," I said.

"Take him back to his room." She wasn't really asking me, but I answered her like she was.

"Sure. I'll grab a cab and be right back."

"See you then."

As I piled Chuck into a taxi and hoped that he didn't vomit on the two block stretch of the Strip that we navigated down, I still thought that maybe I could salvage this night. I could get him down, make sure he wasn't going to choke on his own vomit, and hopefully get back in time to meet up with the crew before they went wherever they were going. If not that, then I had other options—it was a reception for gym reps, and it seemed to be an unwritten rule that they lived by example.

Chuck sank into the seat of the cab, leaning his head back so that he could look out the back window at the desert sky. Light pollution from the gaudy casinos reflected off the clouds, turning night into perpetual twilight.

"Hey, man..." Chuck lost his train of thought, and for a second, I wondered if he'd dozed off, mid-sentence, before he spoke again. "Hey, man, you and Casey ever...?"

It took me a second to realize what the hell he was talking about. "What? No!"

"Okay."

I thought that there might be more to the conversation, but he didn't say anything. Ten seconds later, I actually *did* hear snoring. Casey and I...that was a pretty funny thought, although she did look great tonight. Maybe it could work if I didn't know anything about her beyond that dress, and didn't have to work with her in the morning. But I did, so it couldn't.

The cab pulled up to our hotel.

"We're home." I shook him awake. I'd harbored the vague hope that I'd be able to just drop him off here and let him figure the rest out. Clearly that wasn't an option. Sighing, I paid the cabbie, pulled him out of the car, and led him into the lobby.

"Whoa there, buddy." Chuck stumbled away when I tried to fish his wallet out. "I'm not like that."

I groaned, thinking of all the attractive women at that reception, desperate and ready for a random hook-up.

"Just getting your key. You could only be so lucky to get me."

Getting him into his bed and under the covers was more annoying than I'd anticipated. The abrupt detour to the bathroom—but unfortunately not all the way to the toilet—was part of it.

"Okay, now you're really going to owe me one, asshole." I unbuttoned his vomit-covered shirt and rolled him into bed. Part of me wanted to leave the mess in the bathroom as a reminder, but I ended up cleaning it up. And of course, I couldn't do that without getting some on my own clothes, which meant a trip back to my room to change.

By the time I finally made it back to the reception, all the people I knew were gone. Of course. No Casey. No Linn. And worse, no Tyler Kline.

"They left about a half hour ago."

I turned to see a pretty redhead regarding me, a glass of wine in her hand.

"Your friends left, I mean, if that's who you're looking for." Her green eyes flickered up and down my body as I quickly did the same. Pale skin, a willowy body, nice pair of tits. And most important of all, she was interested.

"All of them together?"

"Most of them did. The woman who'd been talking with Tyler stayed a little longer. They left together about fifteen minutes ago."

The image knocked the wind out of me. Tyler and Linn, smiling at one another as they slipped away. I tasted the coppery bite of desperation boil up from my gut, along with jealousy and regret.

I looked at the redhead, no longer seeing a potential night of fun with her, but the bearer of bad news.

"Thanks. Did they say where?" I wasn't sure what I'd do with that knowledge, but I wanted to know anyway.

"Pretty sure they went up to his room. I'm not a mind-reader, but they were definitely into each other."

God, why did that make me so sick?

"Cool."

"I know some places *we* could go..."

I barely heard her, and didn't reply. Just backed away and left.

I wandered out into the casino proper, floating around like a balloon with its helium nearly depleted. It was pushing ten at night, but inside the sprawl of slot machines and gaming tables, it could have been noon. Out there, a thousand lives played out their own personal dramas, unconcerned with my own.

And what was my own, anyway? That I lusted after a senior executive at my office—someone that I had next to nothing in common with? There were a million reasons that it was stupid: her wedding rings were one; her position another; the awkwardness of working with her after the fact was even better.

More than that, though, we weren't even good for each other. She was used to being the boss—both literally and figuratively—and I wasn't used to giving up control.

Except that I so totally would, for her.

I ignored that voice as effectively as I'd ignored the redhead's veiled offer.

What really got me wasn't that she wasn't with me right now, getting hammered into the bed by my cock. It was that she was with *Tyler*. More than that, that she'd made it clear that she'd chosen Tyler right in front of my face.

I smelled her perfume before I saw her, and felt her soft touch on my shoulder before I heard her.

"Why the long face?"

Linn's accented question emerged like a dream. When I turned to look, I half expected to see nothing but thin air. But there she was, glossy beauty and all.

"Linn? I thought—"

"That I was fucking Tyler?" She smiled at my reaction. "Did I make you jealous?"

Yes. "No."

"That's too bad." She stepped up beside me, looking out over the casino. "I'd like to play some blackjack. Want to keep me company, or do you have better things to do?"

Before I could answer, she went on. "And if some handsome stranger happens to sit next to me, you should know that I'll probably end up taking him back to my room and fucking him until morning." She glanced up at me and I shuddered. "If you don't sit with me, that is."

She was playing me like a virtuoso. I knew it, and could do nothing about it. "Lead the way."

****

"Twenty-one. Winner." The dealer set a stack of red chips in front of Linn. We'd been sitting here for only ten minutes, but she'd already amassed quite a stack, while I was up maybe a few bucks. I wasn't an avid blackjack player, but I'd studied up on betting systems—when to hit, when to stay, when to double down—and had a basic idea of what I was supposed to do.

Linn didn't. Not that I could tell. She hit when I knew that she shouldn't. She took risks that shouldn't have paid off, yet did every time. It wasn't fair.

"You play too safe," she said when I held on a twelve and the dealer was showing five.

"I've got a system."

Her smirk said it all.

"You don't believe in systems?"

She looked up at me with a glitter in her eyes that wasn't there before. "Oh, I do. Systems are great...when you want to be safe. And, I mean, there's nothing wrong with *safe*. But being safe won't get you far in life."

"So you're a risk-taker."

"I like to think about it more like pushing limits." She pointed back to her chips. "That's what blackjack's all about, right? Seeing how close to the line you can get without going over?"

I wasn't a complete idiot. I knew we weren't talking about cards. "Like with Tyler Kline tonight? You two looked pretty cozy." Adrenaline lanced through me.

"You're jealous. I like that."

"You did that on purpose? Flirt with Tyler in front of me?"

"Mmm hmm."

"You're in love with control. Did anyone tell you that?"

"I may have heard it before. But like you said, I also like risk."

"So let's see you give up control."

She raised an eyebrow at me. "You'd like that, wouldn't you?"

"I would, but I'm not talking about giving it up to me. Not in the way you're thinking." I glanced at the cards. "Why don't we let the cards decide?"

"A wager. How setting appropriate, Adam. Go on..."

"First one to get a blackjack gives up control to the other." I glanced at the dealer, a pretty Asian woman who hadn't said a word, but was clearly listening.

"Now that's an interesting idea." She tapped her fingers on her lips in thought. She'd painted her nails a pale pink. "I'm not sure you're ready to make good if you lost."

"I am if you are."

Her eyes tightened at my challenge. "You're on."

"Ready?" the dealer asked, as eager to flip over our next hands as we were.

"Please."

The first few rounds were tense, each turn of the card coming like a mini-drama. Even our dealer seemed to be holding her breath. My shoulders were tight. My thoughts alternated between what I'd do if I won, and how I'd handle it if I lost.

Linn broke the tension in the most unusual way: she apologized. Sort of.

"So about last night..."

"Which part? A lot of things happened last night," I said.

"I'm not sure what came over me. I've never done something like that before."

"Really? Because you were pretty good at it."

"Oh, I know." She flared her eyes.

"But *I* shouldn't know," I said for her. "So what happened?"

She plucked the top chip off her stack and tapped it against the others. "I didn't intend to do that. I was...pushing limits. Things got out of hand."

I resisted the urge to make a quip about how things felt pretty *in hand* for me. Instead, I just nodded.

"I told Mark about it. My husband."

I nearly fell out of my chair. "You what?"

"This morning, I told him..." Linn stopped, looked at the dealer, then went on anyway. "I told him I fooled around with another man in a hot tub last night."

I glanced at the dealer, who wore a smile she couldn't hide.

"What did he say?"

"He didn't believe me. He said that I was making it all up for *him*. That he didn't think I was capable."

Her chirpy laugh sounded bitter.

"That's good, right?"

"Good for you, maybe." She looked at me out of the corner of her eyes. "Now I have something to prove."

The dealer laid down the first cards of our next hand: both aces. I felt the tingle of destiny in that moment, my head inflating like a balloon. We glanced at each other as the dealer dramatically dealt our second cards.

"Twenty-one to the lady. Winner. Eighteen to you, sir." The dealer couldn't help but look excited for Linn. The women exchanged a look that could have been considered conspiratorial were that not impossible.

"I'll stay," I said.

The dealer nodded, turned over her cards, and showed her twenty. I'd lost the hand, and the bet. Chance, it seemed, wasn't shining favorably on me.

"So looks like you're the big winner," I said.

"Oh, don't look so down, Adam. Admit it, part of you was hoping it would turn out this way." To the dealer, Linn said, "What man doesn't want a strong woman to tell him what to do?"

The dealer nodded in agreement, looking at me with a twinkle in her eye. "Enjoy it."

Linn studied me like she would a cut of meat. How would she cook me? How would she eat me?

The dealer was right, I should enjoy this. I didn't love giving up control, but if it meant that I was going to get to fool around with the slender Finn, it seemed worth it.

"This is going to be fun," Linn said at last. Pushing a stack of chips toward the dealer, she slipped out of her chair. When I moved to join her, she held up her hand. "Stay if you'd like. Or go. I'm meeting a friend, and you're definitely not invited."

I was floored. My mind already had us stripping out of our clothes in her hotel room. Now she was standing me up? I checked my phone for the time. "It's 11:30 at night. You're just now meeting up?"

Even as I said it, I felt like an idiot. She wasn't meeting a friend. I thought about Tyler and her tonight and how close they got. Linn hadn't turned him down, she'd only put him off until later, when they were free of all social obligations.

Linn watched me process my own question with a smile, then chose not to answer it. "I'll see you in the morning, Adam. But you're going to start giving up control tonight."

I looked at her sideways as she leaned in, close enough that her next words were just for us. "No playing with yourself. No playing with anyone else. And no coming." Pulling back, she smiled, kissed my cheek, and said, "Good night."

chapter four

I didn't have a good night—or morning. I was too wound up and wasn't allowed to make anything *good* happen. I thought about cheating. About disobeying Linnea's orders and just tugging one out before falling asleep. I certainly had enough material to. Instead, I took a cold shower in the hopes of drowning it all away. That didn't work, either.

Linn was with Tyler right now and that made me want to drive my fist through the shower tiles. That smug prick was lancing his cock in and out of her tight, executive pussy and she was loving it.

I looked down, surprised by the strength of my own erection. I shut the water off, stepped out of the shower dripping, and stared at myself in the mirror.

"Are you thinking of me as you fuck him?" I asked my reflection. Linn had seen all of this the night before, and I knew that she liked what she saw. She liked my muscled shoulders and thick arms. Her eyes had lingered on my chest and the definition in my abs.

And she couldn't get enough of my thick cock. I could still remember the way it felt in her mouth.

I reached out to touch it, then drew back with a sigh. Not tonight. I'd lost the bet. I'd honor it, even if she'd never know.

****

I was up at six in the morning, even with the choppy sleep I managed to cobble together. I still had too much energy and realized that I needed to work it off. If I couldn't do that in the bedroom, I'd have to do it in the gym.

Chuck and I had first shift, although after last night, I wasn't sure if Chuck would make it. Thinking back to that part of the night—the reception and the vomiting and me being a fucking good coworker—felt like recalling a memory from last year. It seemed so long ago.

"Morning, man. How's it going?" Chuck showed up, more chipper than I did.

"Good. You?" I said.

"I don't remember much of last night, but all things considered, I feel pretty damn good."

"Do you remember puking at the reception? Or back in your room?"

"Negative, but that's probably why I feel as good as I do."

"You're an asshole. And you owe me big."

"You got saddled with taking care of me?" Chuck barked a laugh. "You must have pissed someone off."

I didn't want to get into it. I spotted Linnea crossed the convention floor and redirected our attention to her. "Boss incoming."

"With our newest client, too," Chuck said. He was right. Walking at Linn's side was my nemesis: Mr. Tyler Kline. "Oh, they totally banged last night. Look at how they're smiling? They might as well be holding fucking hands."

All the frustration I'd worked off in the gym was back with Chuck's comments, but he was right again. They looked…happy. It felt like I'd been punched in the gut. She'd played me last night, got me all wound up, then left me for another man.

When my imagination started filling in the details of what *left me for another man* meant, I started to harden. Like last night. Jealousy or no, the idea of Linn unleashing her sexuality at all was pretty fucking stimulating.

"Good morning, boys," Linnea said. "Ready for another day?"

"Ready as ever," Chuck said.

I just stared at her. She locked on to me, but didn't concede that anything was different between us. I felt small.

She slid her phone from her bag and handed it to me. "Adam, can you take our photo in front of the booth?"

I grinded my molars as Linnea and Tyler posed in front of the booth. I felt like was chewing glass. Backing up, I framed the two of them in Linn's camera phone. There was nothing cutesy about how they posed. She didn't cock her hip or put an arm around him. For all intents and purposes, they were just two people standing side-by-side in a convention hall.

But see, I had a pretty good idea that this photo would make it into a text to Linn's husband, along with a caption such as *last night's entertainment*. And that burned me up.

"On three. One, two, cheese!"

"Thanks, Adam," Linn winked. She knew exactly what she was doing. "I better run. I'll check in later. Good luck, guys. Just two more days and everything goes back to normal."

The three of us watched Linn go. Today, she wore a sleeveless silk dress, paisley patterned in turquoise and brown. It was less corporate than I was used to, but still professional—short enough to show off her shapely legs and just tight enough that I could make out the shape of each buttock.

Tyler shot me a significant look, one that said, *Remember what I said yesterday? You're a lucky bastard.* Or maybe it was, *I'm a lucky bastard.*

"Gentlemen," he said with a nod, then was gone.

"Yeah, that guy got laid last night. Makes me see Linn in a whole new light," Chuck said.

"Come on," I growled. "Help me pull out these flyers."

****

I started to wonder if I'd either dreamed last night's blackjack bet, or if Linnea decided to exercise her control by tormenting me.

No playing with yourself. No playing with anyone. No coming. As I looked around me at all the fit convention attendees, the significance of that order sunk in. I'd squandered the first three nights in Vegas, and I may be missing out on the last two because of a stupid bet I'd initiated. Not the kind of wild time I'd imagined when thinking of my first trip to Sin City.

"Hey, I'm going to take a walk," I told Chuck. I hadn't done much browsing in the exhibit hall since I'd arrived and the morning downtime seemed as good a time as any.

Being one of the major conventions in the fitness industry, HFC Vegas brought in a lot of big money exhibitors. All the major brands were represented by huge booths that towered over the floor: Nike, Adidas, Under Armor.

Thing was, I didn't see any of the grandiose. None of the money. I saw the women. The booth babes, the regular babes, the attendee babes, the executive babes. All the babes that I wouldn't be sampling. All the possibility, so close yet infinitely out of reach.

A pretty blonde smiled at me as I passed the Red Bull stand, handing me a can. "It gives you wings," she said, and I swear to God she was making eyes at me.

You never determined a time frame for the wager, a voice in my head suggested. It was the same voice that told me last night that Linnea would never know if I took care of myself. This time, I didn't ignore it quite so quickly.

"That therapeutic?" Chuck asked when I returned.

"Something like that." I grabbed my bag from behind the booth. "So I'm calling in that favor now and taking off. Text me if it gets hairy."

Chuck waved me on without protest. "More time for me to flirt with the yogis."

I nodded and walked out, not sure where I was going until I'd changed into my swim trunks and was headed for the outdoor pool. The gambling tables weren't doing much for me, so I figured I could at least work on my tan and soak in some eye-candy. If some of that candy ended up in my room, unwrapped...well, we never established a time frame.

The outdoor pool was serviced by an entirely different set of locker rooms in an entirely different part of the hotel. There was something symbolic there—these lockers were not Linnea Sorenson's, I was once again in my own world. And what a fucking amazing world it was.

So this is the Vegas that I've been missing out on. I almost said it aloud as I watched a couple tight young bodies stroll past me in bright, string bikinis. It wasn't even 11 in the morning and it was packed. A DJ was spinning tunes poolside, drinks were flowing, and I was ready to make up for lost time.

Unsure of what to do and where to go, I settled into an open lounger by the side of the pool, spread out my towel, and stripped out of my shirt. I caught a couple looks my way and smiled to myself, encouraged in my decision.

"Can I get something for you?" The question was delivered by a drop dead gorgeous brunette. She had a soft accent, Russian, maybe, a deep tan, and a black bikini that barely covered her body.

"A margarita. Rocks. Salt." I steadied my eyes on her face, although her pose was designed to tempt me lower. "Thanks."

"Right away."

When she turned, I did look at her, devouring her tight, heart-shaped ass. She had a scrollwork tattoo etched across her lower back that I'd love to see dancing as I fucked her. It wasn't elegant, it wasn't classy, but I was beyond that now. My cock started to rise—something not easily hidden in a pair of swimming trunks. I took a quick seat, pulled out my Kindle, and pretended to read.

Pretended was the operative word here. There was just too much to look at. Not every chick in a bikini was a model, and there was more ink on display than I cared for (and most not as subtle as my Russian server), but it still felt like a never ending parade of hot female flesh.

And then *she* sat down beside me—tall, lean, and tanned with black hair tied back in a high ponytail and designer glasses that just couldn't hide her pretty features. "Hi," she said.

"Hey," I replied, keeping my cool as my gaze slithered over her glossy, oiled skin.

"Anyone sitting here?"

"You."

"And how about on your other side?"

I grinned. "I'm alone. You?"

"Not anymore." The raven-haired beauty settled onto her stomach, reached behind her, and unfastened the clasp of her turquoise bikini top. She held up a bottle of sunblock. "Get my back?"

I checked myself before bridging the gap between our loungers, making sure my cock wasn't too prominent in my shorts. It wasn't at that moment, but I couldn't vouch for the situation in a few minutes.

As I glided my hands across the sinuous expanse of her back, I tried to think of the last time a woman's body had felt this flawless. "You have really nice skin."

"Thanks. You've got really nice hands."

I swept those hands down her lower back, slathering the cream around her slim waist. Her body reminded me of Linn's, I found myself comparing, trim and elegant—although this chick was taller.

"So is this your first time visiting Vegas?" she asked.

"Yeah, my first."

"How're you liking it so far?" She had a husky, inviting voice that made me want to do nasty things to her. Instead, I finished rubbing her down with one last push up her spine, then sat back.

"It's pretty fun. I've been working most of the time. Haven't had much...leisure."

The brunette twisted on the lounger, lowering her sunglasses as she looked up at me over her shoulder. Just behind her, I caught a glimpse of nipple, small and dark brown. While I tried to be subtle about where my eyes travelled, this hottie was brazen as she eyed me up and down. "Hard working man. I like that."

"Something like that."

Her hand brushed across my cock, which was now definitely hard. She said, "Mmm, definitely *hard* working man. Well, I'm glad you're here now. We should do something about your workaholic attitude."

My cock grew in her hand. Her smile widened. It had been so long since I'd gotten off—and I'd been teased too much—that what came next was inevitable. Or would have been.

"For a grand, I can make up for all that lost time. For $1,500, I can invite a friend and give you the true Vegas experience."

I blinked. She was a prostitute? I found that so hard to believe.

She looked more like a fucking supermodel than a sex worker. I balked.

"You're thinking, *how could* she *be an escort*? Am I right?" The brunette didn't wait for an answer. "Honey, before you judge, remember where we are. They don't call it Sin City for nothing, and I *love* to sin. When I saw you come in here and sit down, I thought, *I want to have that.* Perks of my job, sometimes. I get to be choosy on my off-days."

"So what does...a thousand dollars get me?" Jesus, was I really asking this? I'd played the field, sure, but I'd never considered paying for it.

"It gets you an afternoon with me doing whatever you want. I can be your arm candy at dinner. I can blow on your dice at the craps table. We could pretend to be a naughty married couple and pick up one of these slutty co-eds just ready to give it up. If she's hot enough, I'll do her for free."

Right around this point, I spotted one such hottie step out onto the pool proper, pull her cover-up off, and display her impressive rack to everyone who looked. Only she wasn't someone I'd call slutty, and I knew she wasn't a coed. She was Casey.

The escort followed my eyes, a smile forming behind her sunglasses. "Yes, I'd play with her for free. I bet she has a sweet-tasting pussy. What do you think, shaved bald? Or a little something left?"

Thinking about Casey's grooming habits was about the last thing I thought I'd ever do before this trip, and if you'd have asked me before, I would have figured she did nothing special. Now, as I watched her set her things down on the opposite side of the pool wearing a multi-striped, pinkish bikini top, I wasn't so sure.

"I think she's bare, but did it for this Vegas trip," the topless brunette beside me said. "I see that all the time."

My breath caught at the possibility.

"So what do you say? We could start right now. We can do all the transactional stuff on my iPhone. The wonders of technology."

The thought of playing with these two brunettes for the afternoon set my heart racing. And all I needed to do was swipe my credit card and it would be done?

"Don't take this the wrong way—you're crazy hot, and I'm pretty sure you know that..." She inclined her head, affirming that she did. I went on. "But I'm going to have to pass."

I thought about telling her that she was too expensive for my bank account—which was true. $1,000 had been my total gambling budget and I'd already lost more than half of that.

She let me off the hook without needing an excuse.

"Suit yourself, sweetie." She reached into her purse and fished out a card, glossy black with nothing printed on it but a phone number. "I'm booked through the weekend, but if you're ever back in town, give this a call and ask for Nicole. For you, I'd give you a discount."

She fastened her bikini top, sat up, and adjusted the cups across her small breasts. I sighed for what could have been.

"Nice to meet you, Nicole."

She stood, her long body stretching out like a lioness waking from a nap. "Likewise, although I'm not going to lie, it could have gone way beyond *nice*."

There was nothing snarky or sarcastic in her tone. This was business. She'd tried to sell me something, I'd told her no, and it was time to move on. Still, as she sauntered out of the pool area, carrying herself like the embodiment of sexuality, regrets started to creep in.

I silenced it with a quick dive in the pool. I needed to cool off, and I needed to calm down. The chlorinated water was as warm as a bath, but it was still refreshing to twist weightless beneath the surface.

When I came to the surface, I was on the far side of the pool.

Casey stood only ten feet away, slathering sunblock on a body that I still had a hard time believing belonged to my nerdy coworker. Seeing her in a party dress was one thing; seeing her in a bikini blew me away. She was trim in all the right places; curvy in all the rest, from her hips to the flat stomach—surprisingly pierced with a little silver bar—to her large breasts that filled the triangular cups.

I took a few steadying moments to let my cock calm down, then called out to her. "Hey, Case, need some help with your back?"

She looked all around before seeing me in the pool. I hoisted myself out, feeling Casey's eyes dance along my toned upper body as the water streamed away. That look felt nice, but didn't help keep my erection down. I had to hope the water did most of the trick.

"Aren't you supposed to be manning the booth?" she asked.

I walked up and took the sunblock from her. Slathering the coconut lotion in my hands, I directed her to turn around. "I figure Chuck owes me one. It's pretty dead in there anyway."

Casey nodded, turning her back to me. She held her dark hair away from her neck as I rubbed sunblock into the second hot brunette in the last fifteen minutes.

"What's so funny?" Casey asked when she saw my smirk.

"I think I just got propositioned."

"Seriously?" Casey giggled. "This city is fucking crazy. Look around us. Half these people are drunk, and it's not even noon."

Casey had a nice back, with supple skin that felt great beneath my fingers as I layered on the lotion.

"You don't approve?" I asked.

"Oh, no, I didn't say that. Just that this is definitely a city to visit, not to live. I don't think I'd have a liver if I did."

"I'll drink to that."

Casey giggled again. "Speaking of drinks, I think I'm going to join these fine fellows. You in?"

I pointed across the way, where my margarita sat, ice melted and half drunk. "Already started."

"So you told your lady of the night *no*? Or are you meeting up with her later tonight?"

"Come on, I'm not that desperate," I said. "Besides, she was a little out of my price range, although..." I eyed Casey. "She did say she'd do you for free. Maybe we can split her."

"She what?!"

I told Casey an abridged version of the bizarre encounter, loving the way she squirmed. "And based on what I heard about you the other night with the stripper, I'm thinking Nicole may be worth every penny after all."

"As generous as that sounds, I'm gonna have to pass," she said.

"Let me know if you change your mind. I'll be more than willing to facilitate for you."

"Oh, I'm sure you are." She fitted her oversized sunglasses over her eyes—the kind of stylish shades I never would have suspected Casey would own—and started for the poolside bar. "Excuse me, but I need to start chipping away at my sobriety. It's been almost six hours!"

"Aren't you scheduled to work the afternoon shift?" My eyes dropped to her ass before remembering propriety.

"Not anymore. It's great what this whole *feminine wiles* thing can do."

I didn't ask. I didn't want to know. "Have fun. Maybe we'll catch up tonight," I said.

Casey looked me over once, reminding me that I was shirtless. "That could be fun."

I dove back into the water as I started to plump up again. Christ, I needed to get laid.

On the opposite side, I had a text message on my phone. Linnea Sorenson.

–where are you?

It was time stamped 10 minutes ago. I felt like I'd been caught playing hooky—which I kind of was. I decided to go with honesty.

–pool. what's up?

–come to meeting room 50B. be here in ten or I'm going to assume you disobeyed me

chapter five

The convention corridors spread out like a labyrinth, each stretch of meeting space looking like the last. Despite that, I found 50B in 11 minutes. Linn would forgive a minute, right?

"According to my watch, you're late."

Guess not.

"Sorry, got lost."

The room was set for a breakout session of some sort, with enough seating for 100 or more. At the front of the room, up on a small dais, sat two skirted tables and a podium. Behind that, a screen that was currently blank.

"So what did you need me for?" I asked.

Linnea was wearing the same outfit she'd had on this morning, a silk turquoise paisley dress that continued to refine my view of her Director of Ice brand. It was more feminine than the pantsuits she normally sported, but she was also here to sell, not just direct.

"I got asked to participate on a panel. Just this morning," Linn said.

For one short moment, all I could focus on was her exotic accent. Did she moan differently? Did she cry out for more with that accent?

"Are you listening, Adam?"

"Sorry, yes. A panel. Seems easy enough."

"The other panelists are the marketing directors from Reebok, Oakley, and Lululemon," she said, her calm voice starting to fray.

"Oh."

I'd never seen Linnea Sorenson look visibly anxious, although it was subtle. She stood stiffly on stage, her shoulders tight, and kept brushing a strand of imaginary blonde hair out of her eyes.

"Right. *Oh*."

I asked the obvious question. "How's a software development company supposed to compete with those established brands?"

"Actually, I have some ideas." She gestured woodenly to the pad of paper sitting on one of the tables. "That's not why I needed you here."

For some reason, when she looked down at me from up there on the stage, my heart started racing. It was like I knew what came next, yet couldn't quite wrap my brain around it.

"Remember a couple nights ago, I told you how I get when I'm stressed?"

Horny. "Yes…"

"I'm stressed. And I need some relief."

Slow breath. In and out. I wanted to run up there and tackle her. I wanted to pull her slight body into my arms and ravish her mouth as we tore our clothes off. But that's also precisely what she wanted, too, and I hadn't been this pig-headed until now only to throw all my cred away because Linnea Sorenson told me I could finally jump.

"Didn't you get enough last night?" I said instead.

Linnea's eyes flared. She started to relax. This was a game she could play. She sauntered forward, pulling her chair back. It scraped loudly along the hollow dais, reverberating around the empty meeting hall.

"Jealousy. I like that," she said. "You know what my husband said when I sent him the pic you took of me and Tyler this morning? He said, *finally.*"

Linn was right. Jealousy was exactly what I felt. Jealousy so thick I could suffocate in it.

"And you know what?" Linnea said. "I couldn't agree with him more."

She slithered down into the chair, reclined back into it like it was a beach lounger, not a padded conference chair. The pose looked neither comfortable, nor one that fit Linnea Sorenson's persona.

"What are you—"

"This is where you come in, Adam. Don't think I've forgotten about our bet. Time to show you that I really am the boss." She pulled a scrap of turquoise cloth out from beneath the table and held it up. Her thong. "We've got about an hour before my panel starts, but you know how these people are; they show up early to get seats. So let's not waste time."

Her smile said that she owned me. She did.

"Now be a good boy and crawl up under the table. Quickly now, before someone comes in."

Was this really, honestly, fucking happening?! I was a ball of wild emotion. Disbelief, anger, stubbornness, jealousy, and excitement all vied for control. None of them could wrest it away from Linn and that cool, sexy accent.

Giving up control was my saving grace. I had no choice. I did as I was told.

It was hot and dark beneath the table. Linn's aroma filled the confined space, spicy and raw. I could see her legs, poised at the edge of the seat. Crossed. She wasn't making this easy for me.

I started with her knees, savoring the soft skin beneath my lips. I ran my hands up the outside of her thighs, a forward expedition into the new and unknown.

All it took was a gentle pull at her crossed knee and her thighs parted. The smell of her excitement grew stronger. My mouth watered to taste it, but I took my time. Slowly, I pushed the silky skirt of her dress up her thighs. She rose up, sliding right up against the edge of the chair. I crawled in closer.

Linnea Sorenson, object of my lust and unattainable fantasy woman, sat splayed before me, shiny and ready. I'd expected a growth of trimmed hair, or maybe something wild and unmaintained. When I made out the tightly shorn brush of pubic hair above her compact and completely bare pussy lips, I wondered if this fantasy could get any better.

I wanted to drag out the torture, but the sight of her beautiful pussy was too tempting. I needed to taste it. I needed to feel it as I dragged my tongue along those fluted lips.

Linn gasped above me as I lapped her. She gripped the table edge, quickly getting her breathing under control, even as I worked into my rhythm.

I always prided myself on my oral abilities. I loved pleasing women, and it was surprising how many guys balked when it came to this act—yet expected a blowjob without a second thought. I loved hearing a woman moan because of me. I loved knowing that was solely because of me. That it was Linnea Sorenson moaning made the act that much more sweet.

"Oh, Adam...that's...so good."

Her legs folded around me as I lapped along her soft lips. I covered her entire sex with my mouth and drove my tongue deep into her.

She rewarded me with a deep moan that she couldn't quite stifle.

I danced my tongue higher, adding my fingers to the sweet torture. She was so wet that I buried two fingers inside her with little resistance. Hearing her moan above me was almost as good as the memory of her mouth around my cock. I grew as hard as I was that night.

"Uhhh, yes, Adam." Her whisper barely reaching my ears through the skirt of the table and her clamping thighs.

Did Mr. Kline do this for her? Or was he all too eager to fuck her?

The imagined rivalry spurred me on. I pulled the hood of her clit up and criss-crossed its underside as my free hand drove in and out of her. She responded instantly—that trick always worked. I could hear it in the tenor of her moans and the grip of her pussy. I considered backing off—considered leaving her wanting, just as she'd done two nights back. Then her fist tightened in my hair and desperation clung to her cries.

This was Mrs. Linnea Sorenson I was eating out. The Director of Ice was melting in my mouth. Why was I going to stop now?

Twisting my fingers, I stroked them along the textured surface of her g-spot. I pinched her hood and flickered my tongue tip under her clit. "Uh—gah!"

No mercy. I took pleasure in that thought. Linn may have had power over me in every other walk of life—bet or no bet, that was the honest truth of it—but in that moment, with her thighs clamped to me and her pussy quivering on the end of my tongue, she was mine.

I ate her through her orgasm, unable to retreat even if I wanted to. When her legs finally relaxed, I drew back enough to breathe, yet still run my tongue along those enticingly smooth petals of hers.

She released a long sigh, touched my face, and pushed back. "That was just what I needed. Thank you, Adam."

I brushed my face with my shirt sleeve before crawling out from under the table. The balance of power returned to its former self with that gesture—it was hard to straighten up from your knees and make it look like you were in control.

The door clacked open at the other end of the hall, echoing through the room. I'm not sure who jumped more, me or Linn.

"Um, is this 39A? *Next Gen Footwear*?" the guy asked.

Linn and I shared a look, them burst out laughing.

"What?" the guy asked.

"Nothing. I think 39A is next door," Linn answered.

"Great. Thanks!" And the guy was gone.

I took a seat beside the blonde as she straightened her dress. "That was a close call," I said.

Linnea just laughed some more. She even had the grace to blush. More than anything I'd see over the course of these last four days, this was the most humanizing.

"Well, thanks again for taking the edge off." She shuffled her notes in front of her. "The nice thing about representing the unknown brand in the room is that the only way this could go is up."

"Glad I could help." I tipped an imaginary hat, adding: "Again."

"Enough blowing up that ego for now. I'll see you later."

"Later when?" I couldn't help asking, I was on a roll, after all.

"Oh, now we're getting cocky. Have you done as you were told so far?"

"You mean have I kept myself pure for you?"

"Well, we know you haven't been pure," she said with a wink. "But you've resisted the...temptation?"

"Yes, ma'am."

"Don't *ma'am* me, mister, or I'll *young man* you! So when you skipped out on your shift to hang out by the pool, you weren't looking to break that order?"

Busted. "No, of course not," I lied. "Just looking to grab some sun."

"In that case, sun away. In fact, please do. But I'll have my spies watching you. You better not leave with someone special."

"Your spies, huh?"

"Trust me, it's not worth disobeying."

She was still smiling, but I didn't doubt her for a second.

"I think some of the team is headed out tonight," I said. I wasn't sure if that was true, but it felt like the right thing to say in parting. "You in?"

Linn gave me one of those looks, like the flash of headlights moments before being run down. "Thanks, but I've already got dinner plans already."

Nothing more was said. Nothing more had to be. I felt cheap. Here I was, hoping there was more going on between the two of us, and I was dismissed like a bellhop.

"Right. Of course. Well, have fun."

"Oh, I will. But Adam?"

"Yes?"

"Don't stay out too late. I may need some...company when I'm back, in the pool."

Despite the second rate citizen feeling, my heart raced.

"Yes..." I looked up at her. "Ma'am."

Linn's smile tightened. "See you later."

chapter **six**

So, temptation. It was everywhere. I went back to the pool, but didn't last long. It was too difficult to disguise my erection.

I showered, dressed, and hit the tables in the casino next door. This time, I tried out the poker room, playing low-stakes limit poker. Surprise, surprise, I actually won some money. Maybe my luck was turning around.

The slower pace of the game allowed me to think, too, and for the first time, I got some perspective on my situation.

Maybe I wasn't thinking my situation through. This was Las Vegas, where the rules don't apply, and pleasure was as available as it was evanescent. In any other city, exchanging oral favors with a woman of Linnea's station would have made it the trip of a lifetime. That's the lens I needed to be using.

The other great thing about this week was getting to see a side of Casey I'd never known before. Not that looks were everything, but I won't lie, they mean a lot. I'd always regarded her as my cute, but book- ish coworker. Now, I saw her as so much more. Even when I texted her to join me and she showed up in a snug pair of capri jeans and a pink polo shirt, looking like a more familiar Casey than any I'd seen this week, I saw the other, sexier one there, lurking behind her dark-framed glasses.

"So you just hanging out, hoping to get propositioned again?" she said. Her face glowed with her recent dose of sun earlier.

I thought of Linnea in the meeting hall, but managed to keep my face neutral. "You offering?"

"Adam, you couldn't afford me."

I shuffled the chips in front of me. "I'm doing pretty well. What's your price?"

Casey didn't bother looking offended. That's the kind of relationship we had—more brother and sister than anything else. Right?

"Takes more than money to get in these jeans." She glanced down at my cards. "You going to sit on those all day? Or make a bet."

I didn't even realize the table had been waiting on me. "Fold. Sorry."

My luck turned after Casey showed up. The stack of chips I'd built started to shrink, although truth be told, I didn't mind. It was nice to just hang out with Casey.

"So you never come out with us at work," I said at one point. "What's up with that?"

"We went over this. I need you guys to see the mousy coder. That's the way this works. Otherwise, it's *sweetheart* this and *baby* that. It would be having my code checked and doubted. It's a male world, I get that, and this is how I deal with it. No happy hours. No golf outings." She adjusted her nerdy glasses and smiled. "This is what you get."

I'd been drinking comped drinks—even watered down ones— long enough that I just said the next thing. "That's bullshit."

Casey blinked, surprised by my passion, maybe. I went on.

"You're brilliant. You have a degree from MIT, for Godsakes. Anyone who *sweethearts* you is a total jackass."

The guy on the other side of me—a true Vegas local, faded and grizzled—leaned into our conversation. "He's right. I'd never call you sweetheart, doll."

Casey and I looked at each other, uncertain if he was being ironic or not. Deciding that he wasn't, I scooted back until I was in line with the stranger, and regarded Casey with him.

I nodded with him. "With that little nose, round cheeks, and big, blue eyes, I'd say *doll* is pretty accurate, too."

Casey rolled her eyes. "So that about does it for me. I'm out."

She pulled her clear acrylic chip tray and began loading it up. I followed suit, not wanting the company to end for some reason.

"You doing anything now? Want to walk The Strip and grab something for dinner?" I asked.

Casey hesitated, looked past me at the leering gambler, and shrugged. "Why not. You owe me for saving your ass on the City Fitness job."

"Was thinking halfsies," I said. "You don't want me to start seeing you as just a pretty face."

As we left the poker room, Casey leaned in. "You know, it's not that I don't like being...noticed. I just try to separate business from pleasure."

"Right." I nodded. "Don't worry, I can't see past those glasses."

Casey shook her head, muttered something I didn't understand, and walked off into the casino.

****

We floated along the Las Vegas Strip, buoyed by the buzz of drinks and the energy of the crowds around us. Lights lit up the night, a carnival sprawl grown out of control.

We walked without a destination in mind other than food, just enjoying each other's company. My hand twitched to hold her hand. I had to keep reminding myself that she was just a coworker.

Not surprisingly, it was impossible to find somewhere to eat at any of the restaurants on a Thursday night, so we settled into a lounge off of the casino floor of the Bellagio. No grand view of the dancing fountains, but the casino was almost as amusing.

"So how's your Vegas experience shaped up so far?" I asked Casey as we watched an entire group of men dressed as Elvis walk by with racks of chips in their hands.

"Pretty good. This place is a little over the top for me, but I can hang when I need. You?"

"It's been okay. A lot more work than I thought. I feel exhausted all the time," I said.

"Yeah, I've noticed." She took a sip off her long-neck bottle of beer. "Have you even gotten laid?"

I thought of my two close calls with Linnea, but could truthfully answer *no*. Then it occurred to me. "Wait, have you?"

Casey's face lit up. "Uh huh."

I sputtered. "When? Who? Chuck?"

"Chuck? God, no." Casey released a hearty laugh. "Remember that night we got invited to the gym reception with Tyler?"

"Tyler Kline? Of City Fitness, our newest client? *That* Tyler?"

Casey waved it off. "Calm down. He's a buyer. We'll never see him again. Besides, you heard Linn. I'm surprised she didn't sleep with him instead of me based on the way they were carrying on that night."

Wait. If Casey had spent the night with Tyler, that means that Linn did not. Which means that so much of her story had been...a story. I was as fooled as her husband.

Casey misread my contemplation. "Adam, you're not jealous, are you?"

"No. Of course not. Just...surprised."

Casey started to speak when who should show up but the man of infamy himself.

Tyler stood at the entrance of the lounge, valiant and proud, with an equally stunning redhead at his side. His smile spread like bleach across that too perfect face as he recognized us. He held up his meaty hand in a single wave. Even from where we sat, I knew that wave was directed at Casey, not me, and that burned me up.

Tyler and the redhead approached. I rose to meet them like a challenge. Casey stood with me.

"If it isn't my two favorite developers. What a coincidence. We're actually just coming from dinner with Linn."

I didn't like the way he called our boss by her familiar name. I wanted to correct him, to tell him that it was *Linnea Sorenson* to him. Instead, I said, "Definitely crazy coincidence. Small world here."

Tyler nodded, then realized that he hadn't introduced his companion. "I'm sorry. How rude. This is Dana. She's one of the other buyers out here with us."

Glancing at the leggy redhead, recognizing her from the reception. She'd been the one I could have had fun with had my head not been filled with jealousy. "Hello, again," she said.

I cursed our luck getting stuck with Mr. Square Jaw.

"How're you doing, Case?" Tyler asked my coworker, moving on. I exchanged smiles with Dana as the two got reacquainted.

"I'm good. Just enjoying one of the last nights in Vegas," she said. I wasn't loving the way she was going all moony over him. It didn't seem right.

"Another coincidence. So are we." He looked at Casey in a way that caused the hackles on the back of my neck to rise. "Want to enjoy it together?" He looked at me, an afterthought, and added, "All four of us."

I looked again at the redhead, who offered the same promising smile she'd given me last night. "Second chance?" Dana asked me.

My mouth went dry. I glanced at Casey, expecting her looking as shocked as I felt. She was a smart girl, she knew what was going on. What I saw seemed even more shocking. She bit her lip, quickly glanced at me through the side of her dark glasses, then back at Tyler.

"When in Vegas, right?" she said.

I think my mouth dropped open. Dana laughed, and Tyler agreed with Casey with a smile. "You'd mentioned wanting to be outrageous. Here's your chance."

My phone buzzed as the bizarre conversation careened on. I stepped away to check it, already knowing who it had to be. *I'll text you after dinner*, she'd said, and now here we were.

- pool's shower room. 20 min. be naked

Somehow, I kept a straight face. "I actually need to get going. I'm meeting up with someone."

"Oh?" Casey asked, her blue eyes sharp.

"I'll see you in the morning. Have fun." I winked, and Casey had the grace to look bashful.

"Take care, man," Tyler said, clearly not too broken up that the foursome had turned into a threesome. To Casey and Dana, he said, "How about a drink first?"

"Yes, please," Casey said, a bit too quickly.

"Night," I said again, but I was already forgotten. I took my leave. Was my heart beating at the thought of Casey doing what I thought she was about to do? Or what I was about to?

****

Minutes felt like hours as I waited, standing naked in an empty locker room after hours. I could hear Linn's strokes echo in the pool room, but stayed where I was told, letting my thoughts bounce around in my head.

Linn's ruse, that she'd never actually slept with Tyler Kline, was first and foremost. But mixed in was that electric realization that Casey had—and probably was now. It scalded my insides to think about her laughing at something he said and falling for his charms. She deserved better than him.

"There you are." Linn's silky voice from the doorway snapped me back into my own unlikely situation. My jealousy bled away—although it wasn't jealousy—but the pressure remained.

"Here I am." Something hulking shifted inside me, ready to get out. If Linn sensed it, she wasn't intimidated.

The blonde sauntered in, dressed in her black utility bikini that was sexier than it had a right to be. Her hair was still wet, slicked back along her scalp, and her bare skin shimmering in the harsh, fluorescent lights.

"Mmm, just as ordered, too," she said, glancing at my bared cock. "Getting excited for what comes next?"

I just stood there, silently watching as she crossed before me and entered an open shower stall. The water cut on, hissing to life.

"Have you been good, Adam?" she asked, peeling the racerback bikini top over her head.

My eyes skipped along the lines of her back, hard yet still feminine from all the hours spent in the pool. She tossed the bra into a wet pile in the corner and glanced over her shoulder at me. "Have you?"

"Yes."

"No playing around? No flirting with other women?"

Linn watched me carefully as I formed my answer, my thoughts taking a jag over to Casey.

Linn pushed her thumbs into the tight bottoms of her bikini and eased them down her narrow hips. Her ass came into view—the ass I'd caught a glimpse of the other night, clad in a thong—before she drew my attention back to her. "Have you, Adam?"

"No."

Linn shimmied out of the bottoms at last, leaving her completely naked. I caught a flash of pink between her thighs—those smooth lips I'd sampled earlier today—before she straightened up and stepped beneath the hot water.

"Come here, Adam. I don't think you're being entirely honest with me, and we're going to need to do something about that."

Anger pulsed through me. I wasn't being entirely honest?! My cock surged with sudden adrenaline. Blood pounded in my ears.

Linn half turned, her small breasts presented to me on her lean body. For the first time, she saw the fire in me. She took a sharp breath before I crashed over her, scooping her into my arms and doing what I had been dreaming of doing for days.

I kissed her.

She resisted for all of a second, then her lips and mouth were there, too, snapping and gnashing at me. Her fingers twisted into my hair, now wet from the shower, as she pulled me down to her. I tasted chlorine on her lips, along with the sweeter flavor of the woman herself.

Linnea wrestled back control, pushing me away. No more denying each other, I thought, preparing to resist her when she pressed herself against the tiled wall and set her hands on my broad shoulders. "On your knees. This is for lying to me."

My brain was in sex mode. I had no idea what the fuck she was talking about, but I was more than happy to apologize like this. From my knees, she took on the full command of Linnea Sorenson—not the petite executive I'd just been kissing, but the woman who commanded respect.

I traveled her nudity, from the slopes of her high tits with their pale pink nipples to her flat stomach to her shaved pussy and that tab of trimmed hair above. Hard to believe that the reality of this MILF actually surpassed the fantasy.

"God, the way you look at me," she said, more to herself than me. "Do it."

For the second time that day, I dove between Linn's thighs. This time, there was nothing quiet or covert about it. As I raced my tongue up that smooth crease, she lifted a leg over my shoulder, rocked her head back, and cried out. Her moan echoed through the locker room, reverberating in my ears. Driving me on.

My cock brushed along the warm tiled floor as it grew. I was tempted to stroke it, but resisted. Soon, I'd bury it in the sweetness before me. I could deny myself a little longer.

Linn's grip in my hair went from guiding to painful as an orgasm billowed through her. I withdrew my tongue from her clit as she made a fist, licking along her slick folds.

"No, you don't," she said, her voice twisted up in another moan.

I dashed my tongue along that little button before pulling back again. I gasped as pain seared across my scalp.

"No. You. Don't."

If that's what you want...

I drove the heel of my tongue against Linn's clit, closing my lips around as much of her pussy as I could manage, and sucked. Hard. The pull/prode pressure spun her off like a top.

When Linnea finally released me and I was able to look at the heaving form of her climaxing nudity, my cock thundered to full strength. I sat back on my haunches, battered by the shower, and watched her come down from her orgasm. Still pressed against the wall, eyes closed and chest rising and falling in deep, yet unfulfilling breaths, she looked so vulnerable.

I stood before the moment was gone and the balance was back her in favor. Crossing over to her, I pressed my body against hers, pinning her between me and the wall. Dipping low, I nuzzled her neck, feeling her pulse race from the last climax.

Her hands gripped my arms—to push me away? To pull me close? It didn't matter, I was through with games, and through with being denied. Reaching between us, I encircled my cock and positioned it against her slippery open.

I waited for the resistance—searching for signs to tell me no, too far. They didn't come. Her hand traveled over my shoulder to grab the back of my neck. I got the message, pulling back enough to look her in the eyes.

Do me, she demanded. *Fuck me.*

Rolling my hips forward, I obliged.

"Oh, yes!"

I went into her like wet silk, friction without resistance. Pulling Linn's left leg against me, I sank to my balls, holding her to the wall.

"So is it everything you imagined it would be?" Linn asked, her husky voice droning beneath the shower spray.

"I could ask you the same..."

"Mmm..." She wrapped her arms around my neck, then her legs around my back, and leveraged herself against the wall. "Yes. Everything and so much more."

I bounced her in my embrace, flexing my arms to glide her up and down my shaft. My muscles screamed. I dug deep, ignoring the burn. Harder. Faster. I took a page from the endless hammer of the shower around us. Our skin slapped wetly.

"God, baby, you feel so good," I gasped. Our lips found one another, kissing wetly as the water coursed around us. Her cunt was tight, a ring of pliant flesh that raced along my shaft with each bounce.

I thought of the Linn that I'd known before coming to Vegas—the one who stood before the company in her crisp power-suits as she gave an update on what the marketing department had done over the last quarter. I thought of that straight-backed posture and the untouchable professionalism she commanded.

That same woman was here, in my arms, my cock plunging in and out of her shaved pussy. That same woman who was all business fought for breath as her body squeezed around me.

Linn's fingernails bit into my shoulders. Her voice clawed through a curtain of pleasure. "Are you close?"

"So. Close," came my clipped reply.

She nodded, marshaling her strength to unravel her arms and legs and slither down to her knees. I groaned as I slid free, but my disappointment lasted only a moment before Linn's lips wrapped around my length.

That unforgettable feeling from earlier in the week was back, edging me to the brink. When her fingers swirled around my scrotum, I was one hard suck away from exploding.

"Ohmygod!" My orgasm went off, swift and crippling. My knees buckled as I filled Linn's slurping mouth. I caught myself on the wall before I crumpled, throwing my head back and bellowing as I came.

I staggered back, sitting on the edge of the shower stall. Linn sat opposite me, one knee tugged up to her chin as her chest pumped. Her blonde hair looked darker when wet, still pushed back along her head, giving me an unobstructed of her crisp European beauty.

"You're incredible." My words tumbled out before I could stop them.

When Linn smiled, it set off her cheekbones. "Please. I've hung out by the pool, too, you know. I know what my competition is like."

I leaned my head against the entrance of the shower. Despite the steam, the tile was still cool this far from the spray. It felt good. "They've got nothing on you. Don't get me wrong, they're all hot, with nice bodies that they definitely like showing off. But seriously…" How many times could I tell her she was beautiful, or incredible, or amazing, before it lost meaning? "I'd take you over them every single time."

Linn's smile softened. How did she do that? "I think you need to tell me that because I'm your boss."

I shook my head. Drawing myself out of my slump, I crawled through the hot water again and rested against the wall beside Linn. My excitement was starting to fuel round two, although I wanted to be much drier before we got there.

"You do realize that that only makes you hotter, right?"

Linn laughed. "So you're not just here because you lost a bet? Truthfully?"

I looked her in the face—a face so familiar, yet forever changed—and nodded. What guy wouldn't want to be here, naked with his hot, older coworker? With a woman who brokered deals and led multi-million dollar marketing strategies? She was so put together most of the time, and yet I'd just had her screaming my name as I fucked her.

Was I only here because I'd lost a bet? Fuck no.

"Truthfully, there's nowhere I'd rather be."

"What about my room?"

"Okay, maybe there."

"Good, because I'm getting all pruny and I wouldn't want you to get the wrong impression about this older woman."

****

"Uh. Uh. Yes. Yes!" Linn's moans punctuated my long thrusts, encouraging me to fuck her harder. I obliged, my balls swinging against her clit with each long drive. We were right up against the windows, Linn braced on the sill as I fucked her from behind. The Vegas Strip glittered below us, a bright runway of sin and excess.

My eyes refocused on our hazy reflection. Linnea Sorenson's brow was tight, her eyes squeezed down to slits as pain-like pleasure danced across her features. Behind her, I saw myself, naked and sweat-covered, clutching her hips as I pounded her.

"God, baby, you're so fucking hot," I said.

Our eyes met in the reflection, hers heavy-lidded yet alert. I watched her watch me as I surveyed her naked and undulating body. Without clothes and without context, no one would have questioned the two of us like that. We were just two attractive lovers, ready to fuck one more time.

"NGH!" she gasped as I thrust forward.

The walls of her cunt rushed up around me, smothering and satisfying. Even splayed like that, she was tight. My balls slapped against her softness and she grunted. I withdrew all the way to the tip, then lunged again. The impact was louder. Linnea clenched her teeth, nostrils flaring. Again. Smack. Out, then in. Long. Hard. Harder.

"Harder!" she cried. Our skin clapped wetly. The clapping became an applause, joined by Linnea's keening protest and my own huffing that began to overload my senses. I felt her fingers between her legs, first working her clit, then tugging ever-so-gently at my scrotum.

I found her reflection again, her brow furrowed and her mouth open as she raced toward orgasm. I fucked her harder. She squeezed her eyes shut and hung her head between her shoulders as she clenched down.

"How does my cock feel?" I growled. I reached into her soft blonde hair, pulling her head back to look at me in the window. "Am I scratching that itch?" Her eyes rolled wildly with lust, her forehead creased. Closer. Closer. "What was that? I can't hear you!"

"Come… come…" So quiet I thought she was panting.

"What?"

"COME!" she screamed, bucking back into me as she heaved and came.

The Strip before us blurred out, turning into a smear of colorful lights that streaked to the horizon. I gnashed my teeth, my lips curling up into a snarl. With one hand on the small of her back to steady me, the other clutching her hair like reins, I let loose. She shivered beneath me with each pulse. My throat was raw before I realized I'd been yelling.

We settled under the high thread count sheets, naked and comfortable in each others' arms. Linn kept the curtains open and we watched the bright lights dance along the ceiling.

"This thing…what happened tonight…" Linn searched for words in the shifting colors. "This has to be the only time."

I knew it had to be that way—hell, that's usually how I preferred my hookups. Still, why did it have to be that way about Linn? She'd be so close and she was *so* sexy.

I forced the petulance out of my head. "You didn't have fun?"

"Oh, I think we both know that I did." She turned on her side and our eyes met. She laced her fingers through mine, the intimate gesture not making the moment easy. "I'd love to have you on the side, back at home, but it's not fair. To anyone."

"Why not?"

"Well, first of all, remember this?" She flashed her wedding band, shining a light on my guilt. "I'm unavailable. I'm also already old, and a guy like you deserves someone to grow old with."

"Oh, please. Stop calling yourself that. You're amazing and you know it."

"I'm still married."

"You wouldn't leave him for me?" It was a bad joke told in poor taste. I regretted saying it as soon as it left my lips.

Linnea let me off the hook. "I have no idea what you must think about me—nothing good, anyway—at least about marriage and loyalty. But the truth is, I love him…"

She rolled onto her back again. I spooned up beside her, gently cupping a breast without touching her nipple.

"I didn't have a whole lot of experience before I met my husband. My parents were strict. Like, really strict. He came along and…here was a man I could marry…a man my parents would love."

"You regret marrying him?"

"No," she said vehemently. "Like I said, I love him. We've been together for twenty years and I'm still in love with him."

I began to understand. Theirs was a love rooted in history. They had kids together. They had crafted a life and grown together. Changed together. But of course, there was a *but*.

"But our relationship was never a passionate one. Sometimes, I wish I could experience it. Something no-strings. Just once." She glanced at me at of the corner of her eye and smiled. "Then he started bringing up this fantasy—"

"The one where you fuck other guys."

"So eloquently stated, Adam. Have you ever felt that way when you're with someone?"

"Want to share them, you mean?"

"Get turned on at the thought of them being so naughty," Linn said.

I thought of Casey right now—Casey and her threesome with Tyler and that redhead—and as much as it twisted my guts to think about, I felt my cock twitch as well.

Linn's hand was there to feel it.

"Who?" Linn asked, reading me like I'd spoken aloud.

I licked my lips, not wanting to admit to the Casey thing. I seized on the next genuine confession. "You. When you said you were meeting up with Tyler."

Linn smiled. "I never said I was meeting Tyler. I said I was meeting a friend…"

"We both know what you were implying."

"We do," she agreed. "And Tyler is definitely fuckable." Hearing Linnea Sorenson say *fuck* would never get old. "He's who I should be having this fling with. I don't work with him. He's not going to be a constant distraction. And he knows the score when it comes to no-strings."

I scoffed at that last one. "And you don't think I don't?"

Linn touched my face. It would almost be motherly, had she not been giving me a handjob at the same time. "I think you think you do. But I also think there's a lot more to you than the guy you project."

Her cell went off before I could fully digest her statement and formulate a comeback. She dug into her bag, offering me the delectable expanse of her backside, and pulled it out.

"Hello?"

I knew that it was wrong, but her statement was still ringing in my ears like a challenge. I'd show her how much more to me there was. Sliding up behind her, I kissed along her shoulder blade and around her neck.

I heard a muffled voice say something. A man's.

"Oh, hi, sweetheart. Where are you calling from?"

Her husband. She looked over her shoulder at me, her eyes flashing playfully.

"Back from happy hour this late? Hope you've been good…" She laughed at whatever he said. "Actually, we had dinner tonight…yes, just the two of us. It was very romantic."

I reached around, rolling one of her nipples between my fingers. She sighed, having to hold the phone away from her.

"Maybe he's still with me…" She wiggled her butt against me. My erection angled across her pussy, already engorged and ready. "Maybe he's behind me, right now. You'd like that, wouldn't you?"

The other end was an unintelligible mess, but his answer was a distinct *yes*.

"He's touching my breasts now. God, his hands feel so good."

I pinched her nipple, drawing a sigh from the blonde. She reached behind me, finding my cock, and gave it a squeeze. "Yes, he's hard. And nice and big, too. We've already fucked twice, but it feels like he's ready for a third round."

More unintelligible speech. Linn sighed as I sawed my cock along her silky sex. "Maybe I'm telling the truth. Maybe not. Mmm…"

She looked back at me, holding her finger to her lips. *Stay quiet, don't make a sound.* Then she pointed at the nightstand, where the box of condoms sat opened. Christ, she was a naughty one.

"Maybe he's about to fuck me again. Right now. How does that make you feel?"

I rolled away as she teased her husband, pulling out a foil and tearing it open.

"Oh, it's been hard to think about anything but…" Linn said, giving me an up-and-down look. "Yeah, I've been trying to figure out how to get him back inside me since then."

I rolled the rubber onto a cock ready to do nasty things to this MILF as her husband listened.

"Are you touching yourself?" Linn said into the phone as she watched me snap the condom into place. "Do it. I want you to be naked and playing with yourself as I fuck him."

My cock swelled, a little sore from all the activity it was getting after being denied for so long. She shifted further onto her stomach with her knee draped over one leg like she was posing for a Renaissance painting. She rested her head on a pillow as she continued to talk into the phone.

"I'm naked, too, honey," she said. "And he's staring at me. God, it's sexy."

Our eyes met. She wasn't lying. I scooted across the bed and got between her legs. I pulled her hips up until I could see her plump vagina spread in invitation. I skimmed my fingertips along her hips and her athletic derriere. A gentle touch. Almost tender.

"He's touching me now. Touching my butt. Touching my—"

I slipped my cock between her thighs, letting its natural spring push it against her sex. She groaned. I teased her, trolling my rigid flesh along her pussy.

"Oh, gawd—" she cried as I hovered at her velvety entrance. She jerked her hips up and my cock head pushed into her.

At that angle, with her hips nearly touching the mattress, her pussy was tight. Each slow thrust passed across her g-spot, forcing a clipped gasp from the sexy blonde.

"He feels so big," she moaned, still managing her end of the conversation. I continued to keep quiet, keeping up the ruse. I wondered if the guy suspected that his fantasy was really happening—that his cool, composed, and successful wife was not only fucking another man, but fucking a coworker she'd work alongside in the months to come.

"He's doing me from behind. I can...ahh...I can feel his balls swing against my clit each time he…" She had to stop as I picked up speed. "Yeah, right against my clit."

Had she answered a question her husband had? Or was it an order for me? I interpreted it as the latter, fucking her hard enough to clap my scrotum against her soft mound.

"Are you close, baby?" she asked. I wasn't, but the garbled bark in the phone told me that someone else was. "Me, too. Tell me, baby. Is this what you want? Your wife to be naughty? Your wife to be a slut?"

Yes! I heard in the phone. And *oh god!*

"I'm being so bad, honey. I'm going to fuck him all night. I'm going to fuck him until I can't walk straight, and then I'm going to fuck him again."

I rammed her harder as her words sizzled not only down the line, but through my brain. The thought of fucking this fantasy woman all night was a challenge I was up for—way up for.

"Yes!" Her voice cracked. "Ah God!" She was on the brink. "I'm coming, baby. Are you?"

The moans I heard on her phone told the whole story. I clutched Linn's hips, yanking them against me as my cock dove its full eight inches into her.

"Come, Mark. Come—"

I dug my toes into the mattress and pile-drove her into her pillow as she screamed through her orgasm. I could feel her fingers flying over her clit as she got off. I could hear her husband's groans down the line. And when it was over, I was still hard, and still going.

"Mmm, baby, that was really good," she said at last. Her eyes were still shut. Her bangs stuck in clumps to her forehead.

I slowed my thrusts, but didn't stop. I wasn't going to until she begged off, and it didn't seem like that would be anytime soon.

"Maybe," she said in answer to some unheard question. "Or maybe I'm all alone, and I'm making it all up. Don't you wish you knew…?"

She laughed, glancing back at me, her eyes finally open. She had a sly look, her hazel irises glancing up through her long lashes.

"I better go, honey. I've got a long day tomorrow before we leave…" She laughed. "Sure. Maybe I just want some alone time with my lover… Good night, love. Tell the kids I miss them. Bye."

She hung up, tossing her phone away from her, and pulled herself out of my grip. I protested only a moment before she flipped over and spread her legs, offering her splayed pussy to me. I didn't need a verbal invitation. I buried myself into her slick depths before the screen of her phone went dark.

Our mouths came together, tongues swarming at the transgression we'd just experienced. To fuck with her husband while they were on the phone? That was evil, even if he was *in the know.*

"Are you going to tell him the truth?" I asked eventually.

"I haven't decided. I know his fantasy is real, but I think the truth would kill him." We fucked quietly for a moment, establishing an easy, familiar rhythm. "And I'm definitely not going to tell him *who* I was fucking, even if I do tell him that I was. I think that my husband has this idea of a whole affair...we'd carry on, maybe he'd spy on us—I'm not sure. But that is *not* what I want."

The confidence was back.

I felt a relief, too. As much as I enjoyed fucking Linnea and was definitely ready for more, I wasn't sure about anything more. I didn't want anything that could get messy.

"So that's what I am? A one-night stand so you can satisfy your itch?" I made sure to make it sound like the light statement that it was.

She smiled back. "That's about it," she said, tweaking my nose and kissing me lightly. "You're my Mr. No-Strings-Attached. Sorry I didn't let you know, earlier."

"I feel so used," I laughed.

"Besides, something's up between you and Casey and I don't want to get in the way of that."

I stopped moving my hips. "I'm not sure what you're talking about." I could hear the defensiveness in my voice.

"I know you don't, but you will. Just open your eyes, Adam. She's crazy about you."

"She's got a funny way of showing it," I muttered.

"What? Because she fucked Tyler the other night?"

"And tonight," I added.

"Really?" Linn's eyebrows rose at that one.

"Along with his associate, Dana."

"*Really?*"

"And she decided to go with them right after having dinner with me, so I'm not so sure how crazy she is about me."

"Well, you're crazy about her, and here you are, fucking me." She squeezed me with her pussy to emphasize the point. "We're in Vegas, Adam. We're all adults, and no one's spoken for except me. I'm not going to say that *whatever happens in Vegas stays in Vegas*, but you've at least got to take that attitude into account."

She drew me down to her and kissed me. "When we go home, you and I will go back to our regular lives. We'll have some good memories, but you can't build a future on memories. Remember that."

"Okay."

"So she and Dana? Are you sure?"

"Jealous?" I asked.

Linn laughed. "Not really. They kind of put the invitation out to me, too, you know. I'm just surprised. Don't let Casey get away, Adam.

She sounds really fun, and…perfect for you, I'd say."

"Maybe you should play matchmaker. The three of us could make the most of our last night in Vegas. Here, in this room. Tomorrow."

Linn rolled her eyes. "Now you're really fantasizing. Just shut up and fuck me, Mr. No Strings. The future can wait."

chapter **seven**

We fucked twice more before it was time to get up and be adults again. The first was a continuation of the phone session. The second started in the morning, when I woke her by going down on her sweet, shaved pussy. She rode me with extra intensity, knowing that this would probably be the last time she'd feel my cock inside her.

When I left, she was in the shower, humming to herself as her loofah left a trail of suds across her lean frame. She faced away from me, the soapy water skirting the lines of her back. I felt myself stir, nearly stepping to join her.

But I knew it wasn't my place. Not anymore. That day had come and gone. I scanned her nudity one last time, felt my lips curl up, bittersweet, and closed the door quietly between us.

The day dragged. We only had half a day at the booth before everything closed down and people started packing up. Because of that, the entire booth staff was there, Casey included.

She blushed as soon as she saw me, shaking her head in warning: *don't you dare say a word to any of them.*

I just grinned back, although inside, I didn't feel so hot.

When Linnea joined us mid-morning, she was back in the business executive persona—the one I used to think of as the Director of Ice. Her pantsuit was black and tight, her heels bright turquoise to match the pashmina coiled loosely around her neck. I wondered what she wore beneath, knowing it was probably small and sexy. I wondered if I'd ever see her in that state of undress again.

"What?" Casey asked, seeing my smile. She followed my gaze to Linn, who was bending over to pull some flyers from the storage bin, her trousers pulled tight across her ass. Casey rolled her eyes. "You can be such a boy sometimes, you know that?"

"Oh, come on, how can you hold that against me?"

Casey laughed. "I *bet* you'd like me to hold that against you."

"Hey, you've now got more experience in that arena than me."

Casey blushed and looked away, but didn't deny it. Jealousy burned a hole in my gut, even as the thought of my nerdy coworker being so naughty turned me on.

I pressed. "Did you have fun?"

She darted a look at me through her dark-rimmed glasses, a hint of a smile forming. Running her fingers through her loose hair, she nodded. "It was crazy. I've never done anything like that before."

"You're a surprising chick, Casey."

The brunette smiled up at me. "Of course I am. You just never paid attention."

My exchanges with Linnea as we packed were all professional, both of us extra vigilant to keep up appearances. "Did you have a good night?" I asked.

"It was pretty quiet. Yours?"

And yet there was a glow about her that she couldn't mask and I couldn't *not* see.

"And how about tonight?" I asked. "Any plans, or the same as last night?" I willed her to hear my loaded suggestion. We still had one more night in Vegas; why not make the most of it?

Linn pushed her fingers through her blonde hair—hair that hung loose about her shoulders, I realized.

"Haven't decided yet. Tyler asked if I wanted to get together. What do you think?"

Ice lanced through me—a jealous feeling that was becoming all too familiar. *She's not mine. She was never mine.*

I looked around us. We were out of earshot of anyone else. "I think your husband would love the idea."

It made me giddy to make her smile like that. "He definitely would. And no matter what happens, Mark's going to think I went out."

The moment closed around us like an intimate embrace, wrapping us in the secret that only the two of us knew: her husband's fantasy, the truth about us, and that unforgettable moment I could never share with another. Ever.

"Or maybe I'll just stay in," Linn went on. "Swim a few laps after hours. Catch a nice, relaxing shower."

Did I read something in that look? The rising temperature beneath my collar suggested that I had.

"Sounds like a good plan."

"And you, Adam? What are you going to do on your last night in Sin City."

I shrugged. "I'm still fulfilling a bet to someone. I'm waiting to hear what she's got in mind."

Linnea seemed pleased with my answer. "Just waiting around to be told what to do? That doesn't sound like you."

My pants tightened. "I've learned that giving up a little control can be very rewarding."

Linn laughed, the woman behind the executive peeking out.

I glanced over at Casey, who was talking to Chuck, and wondered what she'd say about this setup. Would she roll her eyes and mutter, *you're such a boy?* Would she understand? Or maybe, just maybe, she'd feel that twinge of jealousy that I had when I thought of her own mis-adventures. Could Linn be right about her? Did she really like me?

Our boss saw me looking.

"Stand by, Adam. And keep your phone close."

****

If anyone had told me that I would have spent my last day in Ve-gas—a Friday no less—wandering around completely sober, I wouldn't have believed them. Now that I found myself in that very situation, I couldn't imagine doing anything else.

The past week had been a whirlwind. I could barely think back to the plane trip over, when I'd watched Linnea Sorenson snooze next to me. Felt like a lifetime ago.

I took a cab down to Fremont Street—old Vegas, and wandered beneath the canopy of lights that covered much of the casino-lined av-enue. Despite the glitzy show and the volume of drunks around, it felt more subdued than the Strip, and that fit my mood just fine.

Tomorrow, we'd all be headed home. Regular life. All of this around me would fade. All the glamour would fall away, leaving me... leaving me with what? I'd been a bit player in Linnea Sorenson and her husband's fantasy. I was the Other Man. The extra. She'd go back to eating power lunches and *thinking strategically*, and I'd fall back into a hard-partying code monkey.

Or maybe not. Was it time to grow up? And why did Casey's smil-ing face come to mind when I thought that it was?

Chuck texted me a few times, asking where the hell I was, and if

I wanted to make the rounds at the strip clubs since I'd missed out last Tuesday. I ignored him. Texts were convenient that way. Now if it had been Casey, things would have been different.

I ended up at a craps table in the Horseshoe, throwing dice with a bunch of older guys in suits, ties, and hats. They knew the dealer. They knew the craps lingo. I felt like I'd been transported back to a simpler time, when the rat pack was big and bosses didn't come in the form of "Sexy Blonde Finn."

When I got the text from said Finn, I was happy to be in the present.

–feeling like a dip in the hot tub? come now

****

Navigating through the men's locker room after hours came with no small amount of déjà vu. The smell of soap and chlorine permeated the air. My body shook with anticipation. And the same question that I had three days ago was there: nude or swimming trunks?

Seemed like an easy decision to make after last night, right?

But nothing about this arrangement was easy. Still somber from my Old Vegas wanderings, I pulled my swimsuit on and strolled out into the pool proper for what was most likely the final time.

I was halfway to the raised rim of the hot tub when I realized that I'd been set up. Linn wasn't in that roiling water. Casey was.

To the brunette's credit, she looked about as surprised to see me as I was her.

"Case! What are you—"

"—doing here, Adam?"

We both paused, stared at one another, and started laughing.

Casey was the first to get any words out. "I think we've been set up."

I didn't miss the way she looked me up and down, no matter how quickly she did it. She was submerged to the shoulders, but I could see the top of the striped bikini she'd had on by the pool. *Thank God I'd decided to go with my trunks.*

"Linn get you in here?" I asked.

Casey nodded. "I told her I needed a low-key night after...such a busy week. So she told me to schedule a massage—which was *awesome*—and then meet her up here."

I looked around, wondering if Linn was doing laps in the pool and that I somehow missed her.

"Think she's coming?" I asked.

"I don't think so. Did she tempt you with a dip in the Jacuzzi?"

"Something like that."

Unfortunately, Casey was too sharp to let me off the hook. "Wait a sec, did you come here thinking that you and her…"

I slid into the Jacuzzi, hoping that Casey didn't see the lump in my swimming trunks. "That would be ridiculous."

"Sure would. No offense, Adam, but she's way out of your league."

I couldn't help grinning, or saying the next thing. "I don't know about that."

Casey rolled her eyes. "You know, if you just put the macho guy thing on hold, you can be pretty charming."

"Force of habit."

"Well, we can definitely say that Linn's got an unconventional way of playing matchmaker," Casey said.

"Definitely. That woman likes being in control, that's for sure."

"So what are we going to do about it?"

I couldn't decipher the smile on her face, so I answered with a question of my own. "What do you want to do about it?"

Casey groaned. "Are you going to make me do all the work? Fine,

I'll admit it. I…" She rolled her eyes. "I like you."

When she looked at me, her expression dared me to embarrass her. I wasn't going to do that. I was done with games, too. "Me, too."

"Really?"

I floated across to her side of the pool, my heart in my throat as I realized what I was about to do. Casey sat frozen, watching me with skepticism. Even when I reached out and brushed her cheek with my thumb, she didn't move.

"Really."

Before she could dispel the moment, I kissed her.

I'd spent so much time *not* thinking about kissing Casey that the passion behind it caught me off guard. My toes curled. My pulse broke into a sprint. Suddenly things that never made sense fell into place.

"Wow."

Casey nodded, wide-eyed. "Fuck yeah, *wow*. If you fuck half as well as you kiss, we're about to have a really good night."

Seemed kind of silly to question that conclusion, but I almost spoiled it and asked anyway. Casey rescued me once again by sliding her hand across my cock.

"Mmm, definitely a good night."

I released a nervous laugh. "I'm not sure I could top your last night."

With her free hand, Casey caressed my face. "That's not jealousy I hear, is it? You could have joined us, you know."

Linnea's naked body flashed past my eyes and was gone. "Maybe I wanted our first time to be just the two of us."

"So you have no interest in watching me go down on another woman?"

I didn't even need to answer that one; my cock was enough for Casey.

"So maybe you have a little interest," she said.

"Let's establish our *first time*. Then we can talk future threesomes."

"Sounds like a plan."

Our second kiss was every bit as passionate as our first, only this time, our hands had permission to wander. Mine went straight to those breasts that I'd been imagining all week. I felt her nipples press against the heel of my hand. I needed more. The bikini top came away easily, revealing the contours of her flawless, untanned tits.

"Oh, yes…" Casey moaned as my lips closed around the dusky nipple. I sucked and swirled my tongue as she drove her chest against my mouth. A hand dug through my wet hair, encouraging me to feast. I replaced my mouth with my fingers as I switched tits, pinching the abandoned nipple as she cooed above me.

Casey's free hand didn't remain idle. It had been stroking my abs, drifting lower and lower to my waistband. When I switched back to the first breast, her fingers slipped beneath the trunks and raced along my shaft.

Discovering my bare pubis, Casey said, "You're shaved. You really *are* a man slut."

I pulled off her tits to look up at her. "Hey, I'm not the one fucking our future clients."

"*Current* clients, but fine, you win this round." She kissed me tenderly, then patted the spot outside of the hot tub beside her. "Now let's see it."

The déjà vu was back, although my mind was consumed with other things. I gladly pulled up out of the water and sat at the edge. Casey drifted between my legs and helped me out of my swimming trunks.

She didn't waste any time admiring. With just a quick pump along the taut length, she had me in her mouth. Any and all illusions that I'd had of Casey being sweet and innocent were completely dispelled within seconds of entering her mouth. This chick not only knew how to suck dick, but she knew how to control me, keeping me at the edge.

She attacked the top half of me with spiraling licks and tight, controlled sucks, before moving on to deeper, more powerful bobs. I passed into the back of her throat without pause—something that not many women I'd been with could do—then she pulled back and repeated the cycle again.

"Jesus, Case, we should have done this ages ago."

She pulled off me. "Not what you expected, is it?"

"*Nothing* like what I expected. You're so full of surprises."

"How's this for surprising?" She reached behind her and untied her bikini top. I had an idea about what she was going to do next, but it was still shocking when she rose from the hot tub, full tits in hand, leaned in, and wrapped them around my cock.

I groaned, enveloped in the warmth of her soft, wet cleavage.

"I thought you'd like that." She squeezed her breasts in tight and began to fuck me with them, the moisture of the Jacuzzi mixing with her saliva to provide a smooth glide. "Tyler liked it, too."

She might as well have punched me in the gut, although for whatever reason, it made me want her more. Whatever it was—male ego, testosterone-fueled competitive, or whatever—I didn't just receive the tit-fuck, but pumped my hips to match her undulating chest. Each time my cock emerged from her cleavage, my balls would press against the underside of her tits and send me skating closer to orgasm.

"I'm close." My voice sounded a million miles away.

"Are you going to be able to get it up again?"

I took her question as a challenge. "Count on it."

"Oh don't worry, I am."

She squeezed me one last time with her tits before folding over my cock and swallowing me back down her throat. I held off as long as

I could, but when she played with my balls, I lost it.

Casey swallowed everything I had, sucking me dry. When she released me, I flopped backwards onto the poured concrete deck, gulping for air as Casey giggled and sank into the water.

Casey's voice floated to me like a leaf on the surface of a pool.

I opened my eyes, which I hadn't realized I'd closed. The submerged lights of the pool cast dancing bands of shifting light across the tiled ceiling. Everything was blue.

"You're full of surprises, Case."

"You like my nerdy girl act?"

"I like a lot about you. And yeah, the nerdy girl thing's pretty cute."

I heard her slip out of the water and shifted onto my side. She rose like a swimsuit model, water rushing down her luscious curves.

"Good, because most of that's actually who I am, although I'm not sure I'd consider myself *cute*."

She pulled at the drawstrings of her bikini bottom and I found myself agreeing. "No, not cute. Not all the time, anyway…"

My rambling words petered off as she stripped away the last scraps of her modesty. The call girl's speculation about Casey whispered inside my head: *what do you think, shaved bald? Or a little something left?*

I got my answer before the imaginary voice was finished asking the question. Bare and glistening. Not a curl in sight.

"And you called me a man-slut."

"Oh, Adam," she said in the same tone that usually accompanied an eye-roll. "I never said that was a bad thing."

She crawled on top of me, her lips finding mine again as our bodies entwined. My cock began to stir as she rubbed her smooth pussy along its length. She was wet, and it wasn't just from the Jacuzzi.

"So, man-slut, want to return the favor?"

She didn't wait for me to answer. She just crawled over me, positioning her thighs on either side of my head, and lowered herself onto my face. I opened my mouth to her, rolling my tongue across her swollen sex lips. I could taste her beneath the bite of the chlorine, tangy and a little sweet. When I dipped my tongue between her folds, her flavor grew stronger. Richer. So did her moans.

I curled my hands behind her, cupping the juicy shape of her ass, and drew her closer. She obliged, grinding her pelvis into my face. I fought for breath, shifting up her sex to attack her clit.

She shuddered, falling forward and catching herself with her hands. The new angle gave my fingers an opening. I pushed two into her snatch as I lapped harder at her clit.

"Uh, Adam, you're good at—yes! There. There!"

My cock found new life at the sound of Casey's moans. She shifted above me, sitting up and twisted back. When she wrapped a hand around my shaft, I gasped, breaking contact with her pussy.

"Don't stop," she hissed, squeezing my shaft. "I'm close. Don't you dare stop."

If that's what you want. I took control of her hips, rocking her back and forth across my slashing tongue. She got the message. Bracing herself backwards, one hand still clutching my cock, she rode my face without restraint. I reached up, finding her unfettered tits bouncing in time with her galloping pace. I went for the kill, pinching and twisting her nipples as my tongue thrashed across her mound. Her thighs tightened around my head. Her hand started stroking me faster and harder.

Her climax crested just as I began to worry that I'd lose it first. Her hand was there one moment, then it was gone and her moans were reverberating through the empty poolroom.

This time, it was Casey's turn to fall limply at my side. I arranged her towel beneath us before spooning up behind her. I could feel her heart race where my chest pressed against her back. I held her as her breathing returned to normal.

The view through the windows was almost complete darkness: a nightscape of the Vegas desert. But as we laid there in the dim glow of the pool lights, my eyes adjusted enough to pick out the jagged mountain line on the horizon. The harder I looked, the more details emerged—from just land and sky, to the sprawl of the sleeping Las Vegas suburbs, to the scrublands beyond. If I looked hard enough, I could even see a sprinkling of stars through the glow cast by the city.

"That's so beautiful," Casey said, echoing my thoughts. "It's amazing how much more there is to this city than just the casinos and the clubs."

I agreed. All that stuff on the other side was fantasy—a really fun one, but not real. It was a marketer's dream. I hugged Casey close and kissed her shoulder. "It's funny how much you can miss when something flashy is always there to distract."

Casey shimmied against me, my cock digging against her ass. "We should come up here tomorrow morning and watch the sunrise."

I spoke through my smile. "Are you asking me to spend the night with you?"

"Is that a problem?"

"Not at all."

She rolled into me and wrapped her arms around my neck. "Adam, would you like to spend the night with me?"

"I'd love to."

"There *will* be sex involved."

"Hmm… good sex? Because that could be a deal-breaker."

"I haven't had any complaints."

And I didn't want to wait to get back to the room. Grabbing her hips, I pulled her against me as I rolled onto my back. She smiled as she felt my shaft slide along her sex. Guiding her into position, all it took was a quick upward thrust and I slipped inside her. She curled over me, her mouth slack in a silent gasp. She touched my face as her damp hair fell around us, enclosing us in a world all our own.

"God, you feel so good." She sighed and kissed me slowly as her body adjusted to me.

So do you, I thought. Or maybe I said it. I wasn't sure, and a moment later, when she began to ripple over me, I stopped caring. I'd had a lot of fun in the past. Sex with Linnea Sorenson was a memory I'd go back to for years to come. But like the bright lights of Sin City behind us, it didn't feel real. Not anymore.

Casey closed the gap between us and kissed me, her hips driving into me harder as we raced to finish. Our tongues danced with our bodies. My breath couldn't keep up with the pace. Pinpricks formed at the edges of my visions.

"I'm...close—" I gasped.

"Me too. Wait for me," she breathed. "Wait…"

I ran my hands down the smooth sweep of her, her skin damp not from the Jacuzzi anymore, but from exertion. I found her hips. Her ass. The rise and fall of her body. My balls tightened. I wouldn't be able to hold off much longer, but I craved to share something mutual.

I squeezed down on her cheeks and rocked my head back. "Uh, God, Case. I'm…I'm—"

Her cry shattered whatever I was trying to say. Her pussy tightened around me. She rose one last time, ground down into me, and screamed. "Come now!"

I kept my eyes open long enough to watch her crest above me, her tawny body illuminated by nothing but the dancing lights of the pool and the moon outside. I released a breath that I'd been holding since we first flew in, since the moment that I realized how crazy I was for Casey. I thrust upward, lifting her hips as my come erupted inside her.

She fell into my arms, her breath heavy. I held her close, savoring the feel of our naked bodies touching, my cock shrinking inside of her.

"That was...*amazing*," she said. Her hair, now mostly dry, felt so soft where it draped across my shoulder. She squeezed me. "I haven't come like that in a long time."

"Not even last night?" I asked. Last night was like a sore on the roof of my mouth that I couldn't stop tonguing.

"Believe it or not, no. Last night was a lot of things—definitely crazy—but that was just awesome."

"Yeah."

She was quiet a long moment. "Adam, I like you. I *really* like you. But if you want to have our night and leave it at that, I understand. I'm a grown-up—"

"What are you talking about?"

"I know your reputation. And I'm good with that, really. I just want you to be honest with me."

"Okay, I can do that." I took a deep breath. "When we get back, want to get dinner with me?"

"Are you asking me out on a date?"

"Yeah. We can even grab a movie, too."

Casey giggled. "You realize that this is a little backwards, right?"

"Well, we could pretend what just happened didn't happen. Or, we could go back to my room and do it some more."

"I like that idea." She rose off me. I'd already started to grow hard with the prospect of doing it again. "But let's go to my room instead. I've got better toys than you do."

****

"Jesus. *Jesus!*" Casey's blasphemous cries tumbled over the hum of her vibrator. I couldn't believe how dirty this girl was. I had her on her knees, shoulders and face pressed hard into the mattress. I fucked her from behind, our bodies once again covered in sweat, as she pressed a pocket rocket against her clit.

"God, Case, how can you stand that? Just feeling that buzz through you is driving me—*crazy!*"

She skipped the vibrator off herself and rubbed it against my swinging balls. My body quaked before she swept it back up to her clit.

"Pretty fucking awesome, huh?"

"Just...just don't do that anymore please."

"Want to make me even crazier?" She pulled the vibrator away from her again. I braced for another agonizing touch that never came. Instead, she handed the buzzing wand back to me. "Use this against my ass as you fuck me. That's always really exciting."

My ears burned. My cock burned hotter. When I pressed the vibrator against her asshole, she lasted less than five seconds before screaming through yet another orgasm. I fucked her through her moans, never easing up on her until she was reduced to a quivering mess beneath me.

I switched the vibrator off and flipped her onto her back. Sitting back, I took a moment to enjoy the view. Casey's dark hair had twisted around her face, sticking to her cheek and jaw. Tracking down, once again I couldn't believe she'd secreted this body for so long without me noticing. How was that possible?

"What?" she asked, seeing me looking.

"Just thinking of what an idiot I am."

"You finally figured that out, huh?"

I swept down her flat, tanned stomach, pausing a moment to admire the belly piercing I'd seen from across the pool. "Yeah, but I'm determined to make up for it."

"Start by getting me some water. I'm parched."

I glanced one last time at her pussy, open and ready for me, then up at her. She smiled. "It'll still be there after you get me my water."

I crawled out of bed, my legs sore from all the exercise—both last night and tonight. That soak in the hot tub was long gone. I could feel Casey watching me as I strutted into the bathroom, shoulders back and chest puffed out. It only made me harder.

I downed a glass for myself before refilling it and returning to the bedroom. When I did, Casey had her phone out and was laughing at something on the screen.

"Already bored of me?"

"No, of course not." Her phone buzzed again and she covered her mouth, giggling again. "Tyler wants me to come up to his room."

My blood ran cold. "And?"

"And he's being very convincing." She turned the phone to me, flashing me a picture I couldn't quite make out.

I sat at the edge of the bed, my gut twisting with jealousy. When I realized what was actually on the screen, I relaxed. It wasn't a photo of Tyler—or even of Tyler and Casey from last night, as I was dreading. It was of a naked woman, sprawled out on a bed identical to the one we were on. Her face wasn't shown, but I wasn't looking at her face. Her skin was pale, her breasts small but well-proportioned to her slim body, and brushing along her shoulders, just at the edge of the frame, was a loop of copper hair.

"Dana?" I asked.

"See what you missed?"

"Do you want to go?" I realized in that moment that if she said yes, that I'd let her—that I'd even forgive her. We weren't a couple yet, but it was more than that. I looked into her eyes—those deep, pale blues—and realized that not everything was black-and-white. There was a world of gray between a one-night-stand and a relationship. I thought of Linnea Sorenson and her husband—and what the two of us shared. I thought of this whole city, built on a mirage. And I thought of Casey letting her wild side out with a man and a woman that she may never see again. That thought alone had me flushed.

"You listening, Adam?"

I wasn't. "Sorry, what did you say?"

The brunette reached out and wrapped her hand around my cock. "Why would I want to go when I've got so much entertainment right here." She opened her legs. I didn't need any more encouragement.

The phone buzzed beside us. I looked reflexively, catching the close-up of a cock buried inside a pussy topped with a narrow bar of auburn curls. I gasped, right along with Casey.

"Tempted?" I asked.

"Only a little," she admitted.

I fucked her harder, like her confession was a challenge to be met. She wrapped her hand around my neck and pulled me down until I loomed over her, one hand braced at her side.

"Adam, there's nowhere I'd rather be."

I nodded. Her words were like gasoline on a campfire. I took her swiftly, smothering her beneath me.

"Yes, oh yes," she moaned. "Give it—to me!"

I fucked her harder, pouring the last scraps of energy I had into my driving hips. She arched back, presenting the mouth-watering landscape of full tits and slender waist to me. She bucked harder, crying out as she thrashed.

"I want to feel it, Adam. I want to feel you fill me."

Her heels dug into me as I blurred past the point of no return.

"I want to feel you come. Now. Now!"

My climax overwhelmed me, a heady thrum driven home by our slapping bodies and tangled moans. I rammed home one last time, our pubic bones grinding as I emptied the last of myself into her depths.

Casey cried out with me, joining me as our minds spilled out into the dark and unformed horizon.

We cuddled in the aftermath, snuggling beneath the sheets in the dark confines of her room. "Your phone's finally silent."

"Guess they got the message." She giggled. "You're not upset about last night, are you?"

I thought about my night with Linn again. How could I be upset? "No."

"Be honest, Adam. I want us to start off completely open with each other."

I liked the idea of an *us*. I took a deep breath. "Honesty. Okay. Yes, the thought of you sleeping with another dude makes me jealous, even though I know we're not, you know, a couple."

She brushed her fingers through my hair. "Yet."

"A part of me gets kind of turned on, too. I like that you've got this wild streak in you."

Casey glanced at the vibrator on the nightstand and flushed. "Well, like I said, I'm probably more the girl you thought I was before Vegas than the one from last night."

"Right. That right there is awesome. I love your confidence. And that you can get a little freaky, but mostly you're not."

She giggled. "*You've got potential, kid,*" she said in a funny voice.

This next part was hard. It required a deeper breath than normal. "Besides, how could I be too upset about what you did last night when I spent mine with Linn?"

Casey laughed at first, not believing. When I didn't come out and say *just kidding*, that laughter died out, replaced with an incredulous, "Shut the fuck up. Seriously? You and Linnea Sorenson?"

I just looked sheepish and said, "You can't tell anyone."

"Who would believe me!?"

"Hey now, you're starting to hurt my feelings."

Casey kissed me. "Oh, don't be a baby. You know what I mean. She's not known as the Director of Ice for no reason."

I'd forgotten about that nickname. Seemed so long ago when it still applied.

"Are you okay with that?" I asked.

The brunette grinned. "Well, I'm a little envious that she got to you first, but...wait, so when you met me in the pool, you thought you were going to get more director sex!"

"Kind of, yeah."

"Hope you're not disappointed." Her sly smile told me that she knew that I wasn't.

"It was a pleasant surprise—"

"Orchestrated by our boss," Casey added. "Damn, I still can't believe you and her…"

"Honestly, me either."

She looked up at me. "Was it a one-time thing, or…"

"Pretty sure it was a one-time, crazy Vegas thing."

Her hand found my cock beginning to stir. "Too bad. She would have been fun for us to play with…oh, you like that idea!"

I grew hard enough for her to stroke. "What happened to *more like the girl you were*?"

Casey giggled. "I've probably had a crush on Linn as long as I've had one on you. Was she good?"

"This doesn't make you jealous?"

"Not unless you're going to run off and fall in love with her." She squeezed her fingers tighter, bringing back to improbable life. "So *was* she good?"

"Yes." I groaned, thinking back to last night. "You know how some people look better in clothes than not? She isn't one of them."

"She's so fit," Casey agreed. "Did you do it at the pool?"

"Showers, actually. Then her room."

Casey laughed, incredulous. "God, that's awesome." She touched my arm, squeezing my biceps. "I bet you looked fucking hot, powering over her. You have no idea how much I'd love to see that."

"You're a special one, Case."

She flashed me a smile. "What? None of your other girlfriends wanted to watch you fuck their hot bosses?"

"I've haven't had many *girlfriends*. But no. Never."

"Good thing you met me, then." She kissed over my chest and down the side of my ribs. "Did Linnea Sorenson suck your cock?"

I thought of the blonde MILF in the hot tub, hair pushed back, lips wrapped around my erection.

"Yes."

"Hot." Casey kissed lower. "I want you to show me exactly what you two did in her hotel room."

When Casey closed her mouth around my rising erection, I tried to picture Linn's glossy lips down there, her crisp cheekbones and luminous, hazel eyes fixed on me as she bobbed. But the real thing was so much sexier. Seeing Casey slide along my length was all I needed—was all I wanted.

Epilogue

Casey and I didn't get much sleep that night, although we didn't fuck all night, either. After I recreated my evening with Linnea with her and we caught a quick nap, we went down to the poker tables again. At last, my luck turned around. I didn't recoup all of my losses, but it was still nice to win. Casey continued to impress with her skills, at one point charming all of the old Vegas grinders with her soft smile and cute banter.

Cashing out for the last time, we *did* end up watching the sunrise in the upstairs pool. It was glorious. After that, I'd like to say that we went back to her room and made love until we had to check-out, but neither of us had anything to give. Spent and blissfully exhausted, we crashed in bed and slept late into the morning.

In the shower, we used soap as an excuse to rub our hands over each other. My plane flew out at noon. Casey was here until the evening.

"So what are you going to do with you last afternoon in Vegas?" I asked.

Casey slid down to her knees and wrapped her soapy hands around my cock.

"Without this thing within reach? I'm going to lock myself in my room and cry."

"Smart ass."

Casey rotated her hands in opposite directions, working the soap into my length with agonizing efficiency.

"Or maybe I'll see if Tyler Kline and Dana are still around."

Even as my chest tightened and my lungs clutched, my cock sprang in her grip. She looked up at me, a knowing smile tugging up the corners of her lips.

"Does that idea turn you on?"

"I...I don't know."

"Should I start calling you Mr. Sorenson?" she asked. I'd filled her in on Linn's marital arrangement and was surprised when she didn't balk.

"I don't think I'm ready for that."

Casey shifted her left hand down to my balls, giving her right room to really stroke me.

"Maybe I could just hang out by the pool in my little bikini. Think I could score some hot stud there?"

It became harder to breath. Confusion blotted an oily smear on my emotions.

"Yes, I do."

She pushed me back beneath the water, rinsing the soap from my crotch.

"Don't worry, Adam, I'll be good." She sucked me into her mouth, pumping once before pulling off. "I'll only be bad for you."

She ran her tongue up the outside of my shaft, swallowed just the tip and swirled, then licked back down. As if to prove how bad she could be, she pushed my cock against my stomach and wrapped her lips around my balls.

My fingers went into her dark hair, encouraging her. "God, baby, that's so good."

Pulling off, she pouted. "Aw. I was going for so bad." She lapped at my clean shaven balls. "The last time I did this in the shower, Dana was sucking Tyler's cock while I sucked his balls. Now *that* was bad."

I wasn't sure what was hotter, the thought of her and Dana doubling up, or her being naughty with Tyler.

"And when he came, you know what that nasty slut did? She kissed me with his full load in her mouth."

Casey went back to sucking my shaft, pulling off every few bobs to continue her titillating narrative.

"Maybe when we're home, we can recreate that scene...with Linn. Think she'd suck your balls as I did this?"

When Casey returned to my cock, she took me into her throat, swallowing to the root. I nearly lost it. With her fingers simulating Linn on my balls, I would have had I not pushed her away and back up against the tile.

Casey sat back on her heels and smiled. "Too much?"

"I've got less than an hour left before I need to get out of here. I'm not going to waste it on a blowjob."

"Sounds good to me." She stood and shut off the water. "Let's go back to your room. Sounds like we've got a little time to break it in."

****

Once again, Linnea and I shared a plane ride home. The flight wasn't nearly as full as the one out here and we were able to choose our seats toward the back, next to one another. She was pulled together once again, the casual version of the powerful exec back home. She wore a tight pair of dark jeans and a knit blouse with wide, horizontal stripes that alternated white and blue.

"You look tired," she said with a smile. "Did you get to my text?"

Like everything that happened this week, that text felt like an age ago.

"You set us up."

"You two needed some pushing. I was getting frustrated watching you guys flounder."

"You've got a funny way of showing your frustration," I said.

"So what did you think of Las Vegas? Was it as wild as you thought it would be?"

Last week, I would have flinched at that intimidating stare. I would have felt like the subordinate that I was. Now, all I saw was a challenge to meet. I put on my most confident smile and nodded. "Parts of it definitely were. You?"

"This wasn't my first trip to Vegas, Adam, but…it was definitely my most exciting."

"So did you end up going out last night with Tyler Kline?" I asked, knowing that she hadn't, no matter what she said. Surprisingly, she answered honestly.

"I didn't, no. I stayed in my room, ordered some room service, and went to bed early. The pool was occupied, so I didn't even get my swim in." She winked.

"You could have joined us."

She released a crisp, musical laugh. "You two looked like you were having enough fun without me."

It took me a good two seconds for the meaning of her words to sink in. "Wait, you…you watched?"

Linn actually looked away, not quite blushing, but coming as close as I'd ever seen. I'd never be able to think of her as anything associated with *ice* again.

"I couldn't help myself. I was just going to check and see if you two had cleared out. When I heard the moans…" She shook her head and finally looked back at me, daring me to judge. "I had to look."

"How much did you see?"

"Enough to know that I made the right choice," she said.

I tilted my head. "The right choice?"

"You two should have gotten together a long time ago. You're right for each other."

Her words spread a warmth through me that made me smile. But there was something else. "So what about Thursday night? If you thought Casey and I should get together, why did…" I couldn't even say it aloud.

Linn helped me out.

"Why did I fuck you all night?" She smirked when my face went red. "I don't know. I'm not perfect? I'm an opportunist? This was my one and only chance. In a couple years, you and Casey will be married and exclusive and I'll just be an old woman with a fantasy. I wanted to have a nice memory to go with that fantasy."

"First of all, you're not *old*." *And second of all, I'm not so sure about the exclusive part with me and Casey,* I couldn't add.

"I'm not as young as you, either, and I could never compete with Casey—and most importantly, I wouldn't want to. As much as I like the idea of having a hot boyfriend on the side—one that my husband even supports—I'd never want to keep you from living your life. I'm not going to leave Mark, so it just wouldn't be fair."

"So does that mean I'm released from our bet?"

"That you give up control with me? No, but I'll pass the reins on to Casey. Treat her well. I have a good feeling about you two."

"Thanks, Linn. For everything. I've got a pretty good feeling about us, too."

About the Author

I'm just a guy who writes what I like to read: steamy, explicit erotica that's just crazy enough to be true. I write romantic erotica. I write about characters that I like, and endings that feel natural. I write stories where husbands watch their wives get naughty. I write about MILFs and erotic games and loss of innocence. I believe in a world where men read and appreciate erotica, and hope to contribute to it word by word.

Find me online at www.kennywriter.com, or follow me on Twitter at @kennywriter.

Q&A with Kenny Wright

Will there be a sequel?

Once upon a time, I would have given a big, fat no. Now? Well, it's certainly possible. Casey and Adam have a lot more adventure ahead of them. Their story has only just begun, and I can easily see a series of loosely connected stories revolving around them (and possibly including Linnea Sorenson, who knows).

How do I make that sequel and/or series happen?

I've always found that the most straight-forward approach works best: just ask. You can find me on Twitter (@kennywriter) or email me at kennywright.writer@gmail.com. I'm pretty good about responding, so don't be shy. Alternatively (and awesomely), you could leave a review wherever you purchased the book and slip in the request.

Want to acknowledge anyone for this book?

Of course! Big thanks to Max Sebastian and Kirsten McCurran, two awesome authors who are always great to bounce ideas off of. I have to tip my hat to the city of Las Vegas for continuing to be ridiculous (in both good and bad ways); this book wouldn't be quite the same without you doing your thing. Thanks to my editor, Lucy V. Morgan, who does far more than just dot my I's and cross my T's. Special thanks to Stephen Rudolph for his continued support. I will always be indebted to my wife for giving me the time to write, as well as lending some sexy inspiration along the way (you all need to be thanking her, too!). And, of course, I offer my genuine thanks to you, my readers, for supporting me; I can honestly say that I don't think I'd still be publishing books if it weren't for you.

So what's next?

I've got three major books in the pipeline for late 2013/early 2014. The closest to publication is a soft cuckold romance (yes, I made that genre up), called *Training to Love It*. If you liked *Just Watch Me* and *Something Forbidden*, you'll like this one. It's got a strong female protagonist, a hot and handsome personal trainer, and a husband learning just how turned on he gets when the other two play. I added "soft" because there's really no humiliation or wimpy husband in it—things common to the cuckold fantasy but not mine.

After that, I've got a winter-themed book about two couples trapped inside during a blizzard—two couples on the brink of an exciting sexual adventure.

And I'm still sitting on Ian's side of the story of Kirsten McCurran's *Because He's Watching*.

Sounds great! How can I stay up-to-date?

Keep your eye on kennywriter.com. I post updates there with some regularity. Also, find me on Twitter and Facebook.

Your books are awesome. How can I show my appreciation?

Why thank you! The best way is to tell others about me, whether through reviews wherever you purchased the book or on your blog, through social media, or plain old word of mouth (some people still do that, right?). Don't want to be quite so public? Send me an email. I love email!

Something Forbidden (Published October 2013)

Wife-watching. Swinging. Consensual infidelity. These are not concepts that Maxwell Callahan understands, let alone fantasizes about. Max has a great life: husband, father, successful bar owner. He has no plans to shake it up.

And then he witnesses a couple play a dangerous game of pick-up in his bar: the wife gets picked up, the husband watches. A seed takes root and starts to grow. What would it be like to watch his beautiful wife, Katie, in the same situation?

Smart, successful, yet a little conservative, he never thought Katie would ever entertain such an idea…until she does. This suburban couple is about to take a wild ride as they turn fantasy into reality. Don't miss this marital adventure as Katie and Max try something forbidden.

Just Watch Me (Published April 2013)

Dean and Danielle have been playing their game for the past year now: they'd enter a bar as strangers and see what happens. Sometimes, Dean "picked" her up. Other times, he sat back and watched her flirt with other men. And every time, they ended the night together, their passion rekindled.

Jealousy and excitement warred within Dean, but the thrill was becoming too great to ignore. For Danielle, the game had awoken feelings within her she thought long buried–feelings that scared as much as they excited.

Then came the Hawaii trip. Hundreds of miles from home, was this the opportunity to take things further than they'd ever dared?

When a stranger approaches Danielle at the swanky bar, full of surfer-swagger and sun-kissed good looks, the answer was clear.

All In: Strip Poker Done Right (Published March 2013)

Play strip poker? Ben never thought he would. Not with his wife, Amy, and especially not with their asshole friend, Scott. Lawyers all three, they were more likely to strip their opponents of pride, not clothing.

Not that Ben wasn't intrigued—especially in the company of two attractive couples with a history of flirtation. He'd love to see either woman naked; he just wasn't sure how he felt about the guys ogling his wife. But when the wine begins to flow, inhibitions loosen, and clothes start coming off, he discovers a part of himself that's turned on by the attention Amy commands.

Soon, the three couples are caught in the throes of high-stakes poker. Secrets come out, things get wild, and Ben discovers a side of his wife he never knew existed.

Leap (Published August 2012)

On February 29, a day that comes just once every four years, Jack Carter announces that, "What happens on Leap Day stays on Leap Day." His wife Sarah knows he's up to something, and when he explains that today is a day to take risks and get a little crazy, she grasps what it is: he wants to watch her with another man.

Jack had the fantasy first; and at first, Sarah didn't understand it. Hell, neither did Jack. All he knew was that the thought of his wife in the arms of another man was exciting; the build-up, the flirtation, the act, even his nauseous jealousy always got him hard. Sarah didn't deny her own arousal, especially when her coworker, David, began taking the role of imagined lover. He was fit, hot, and most importantly, he was attracted to her.

Neither Jack nor Sarah ever thought they'd take the plunge from reality to fantasy. It was too risky. Too crazy. With February 29 just beginning, will it be the day they finally make the leap?

Also by Kenny Wright

After School Special (A Short)
Eight Hundred Dollar Heels (A Short)
Moving Mrs. Mitchell (A Short)
Naughty But Nice (A Short)
Rediscovering Danielle (A Short)
While She Watches

For a full list of titles, along with their covers, synopses, and where to purchase, go to www.kennywriter.com/books.